DEATH IN THE VESTRY

Also by Humphrey Clucas:

Poetry

Gods & Mortals (Peterloo Poets)
Unfashionable Song (Hippopotamus Press)
Scatter the Darkness: Cathedral Poems (The Lewin Press)

Translation

Versions of Catullus (Agenda Editions, re-issued by
Hippopotamus Press)

Essays

Through Time and Place to Roam: Essays on A.E.Housman
(Salzburg University Press)

Memoirs

Taking Stock: The First Sixty Years (The Lewin Press)

Fiction

Royal and Peculiar (with poems by Anne Middleton)
(The Lewin Press)

Death in the Vestry

and other stories

by

Humphrey Clucas

The Lewin Press

British Library Cataloguing in Publication Data
A catalogue record for this book is available from the
British Library

ISBN 978-0-9550470-3-9

Typeset by Amolibros, Milverton, Somerset
This book production has been managed by Amolibros
Printed and bound by T J I Digital, Padstow, Cornwall, UK

CONTENTS

Original artwork by Janet Clucas

ELEGIES

One

DEATH IN THE VESTRY

IT HAD been raining earlier, but the sky had cleared, and it was a fine September evening as Geoffrey Haygarth walked up the cobbled path towards the church porch. Moss grew between the cobbles, which were uneven and rather slippery. Geoffrey remembered how Margery had disliked cobbles. He had given her a first, tentative kiss on the cobbles outside his old Cambridge college, all those years ago, and had felt warmly about cobbles ever since. But they did not suit small feet, or feminine shoes. Or old people. Most of the congregation was old – over fifty, anyway. The average congregation was fifteen.

Geoffrey and Margery had moved to the village of Little Westing on Geoffrey's retirement, and had immediately been drawn to the church. It stood on one side of the village green, opposite the shop; they were the only buildings in the village which were not domestic. The church was small and mediaeval, with later alterations and additions, but still with a particularly fine fifteenth century wooden choir screen, dividing the nave from the chancel. Geoffrey, who had spent most of his life teaching music in secondary schools, had been an indefatigable pianist, but in his youth, the organ was his instrument. Soon enough, he became the Little Westing village organist. The organ had one manual, six stops, an unusable pedal board and a number of eccentricities, but it gave him a role, and a focus for his week. Margery soon had several; she was on the Parish Church Council, the Village Hall Committee, the Fete Committee... They were glad to have her; there were few enough willing and active people to go round. And then after six years she had died, and Geoffrey was left to soldier on, as one must.

That was four years ago. Now, he was on his way to Compline. Midweek Compline had been a Little Westing tradition from well before Geoffrey's time. Under the Benedictine rule, Compline had been at 6 p.m., after which the monks enjoyed a period of rest till Mattins at midnight, the start of the new day. Little Westing Compline was at seven, followed (in Geoffrey's case) by a large gin and tonic, and a glass of wine with his supper. It was a peaceful service, which took about fifteen minutes. Or it was peaceful when they ran it themselves, which they preferred. It was less so when, as tonight, the lady team vicar was taking it.

Opinion in Little Westing had been ambivalent about the idea of a woman priest. The Parish Church Council was in favour, by four votes to three, but as the new incumbent was to run six churches – Little Westing one of the smallest – and four of the other five wanted her, Little Westing's opinion made little difference. Of the two churchwardens, one, Nigel Martin, had voted for her. Nigel was in his forties, a solicitor's clerk who worked in the county town. He was a small, neat man with short dark hair and a carefully courteous manner; he almost always appeared formally dressed. He was the church treasurer, and his legal knowledge made him useful in other ways. The second churchwarden, Major Henry Thornton, M.C. (regular army, retired) was not so sure. His concern seemed to be less theological than on a rather Victorian feeling that men should run things while women stayed in the background giving support. It was certainly the pattern of his own marriage. Henry Thornton was tall and big-boned; he had swept-back white hair, thinning now, a reddish face, and clear blue eyes which gave you a straight look. In the end, he made no formal objection; as he said, priests were in such short supply that beggars couldn't be choosers.

Geoffrey remembered a conversation in the village shop. Abel Trevissick, a long-exiled Cornishman, had been saying that his brother's church, 'down west', had a woman priest. "They didn't fancy it at first," he was saying, "but after a bit, they found they liked 'er; she be all right."

"That's just male prejudice," said Alice Thompson, who was paying old Paddy at the till. "Suppose your brother had said, 'We didn't fancy the idea of a *black* priest, but then we found we liked him'. You can't say that sort of thing these days. So why does your brother think he can say it about a woman?" And she stepped briskly out of the shop with her basket.

Alice Thompson was a sturdy, plain woman of about seventy, Geoffrey supposed – his own age. She was unmarried. She wore shapeless tweed skirts and cardigans, with thick stockings and lace-up shoes, and usually appeared out of doors in what in the 1960's would have been thought a sensible felt hat. She did not mean to be argumentative; she just said what she thought, with all the assurance of the upper middle classes of her youth – though she was now in what Geoffrey thought of as 'reduced circumstances'. She had befriended Geoffrey after Margery died; he usually went to supper once a month.

"Well now, Abel," said Paddy the small, slightly stage-Irish gnome of a shopkeeper, "you weren't expecting *that* at all at all."

Abel, large and round-faced, was reacting rather slowly; he was a slow man. "I suppose she's right, m'dear," he said at last. He seemed to take no offence. Abel was in his fifties; though a carpenter by trade, he had the look of a P.C.Plod; he was, in fact, also a Special Constable.

Alice *was* right, Geoffrey realised. Either you took the position that there was no such thing as a woman priest, or

5

you had to accept, these days, that women could do anything that men could. Merely not liking the idea was, as Alice insisted, prejudice.

Geoffrey's first acquaintance with the Reverend Abigail Lee was on the May Bank Holiday – tea in the Village Hall after maypole dancing. She had yet to take a service at Little Westing. She was in her early forties, above medium height, with slightly frizzy auburn hair, and a freckled complexion. She had been a teacher before training for the ministry.

"Don't you find those old pews and the screen very restrictive?" she said, almost as soon as they had been introduced. "I shall stand in front of the screen, of course, but I think we could take some of the pews out. Chairs in a circle are so much more inclusive. It's what I find works best in my churches."

Geoffrey made deprecatory noises about carved pew-ends, and aesthetic effect; she listened patiently, a little pityingly, he thought. She clearly saw him as old and resistant to change. But then so many of them were old. The phrase 'my churches' had jarred, too. He had had a headmaster once who referred to 'my school'. No one liked him.

Two days later, she came to Compline; it was to be followed by her first Parish Church Council meeting. She read the service as though unfamiliar with it – which did not stop her telling them what to do. Compline was a said service, but they always sang the plainsong hymn, *Before the ending of the day*, unaccompanied. Abel Trevissick led them off; he had a strong bass voice and sang in a local choral society. The others, as was their wont, tagged along in his wake. After two lines, she stopped them.

"No, no," she said, "it's far too loud – most irreverent. We'll start it again, quietly." Abel was staggered into near-silence, and they stumbled through to the end.

"I almost walked out on 'er, m'dear," he said to Geoffrey

afterwards; a placid man, he was as near upset as Geoffrey had ever seen him.

Geoffrey was not on the PCC; he had had enough of committees. But Alice was, and she gave him the gist of it. The Reverend Abigail Lee, it seemed, was to be consulted about everything; it must all go through her. But Saturday was to be her day off, and no one was to contact her then. There was a certain illogicality about this.

Next, she turned to the services. Little Westing had always had an eclectic approach to its single Sunday service: one Book of Common Prayer Eucharist a month, one from the Alternative Service Book (later, Common Worship), one BCP Matins, and a more informal, lay-led Family Service. This had the odd effect that they exchanged the Peace at one Eucharist, but not at the other. It was an attempt, though, to suit everybody.

"The Book of Common Prayer must go," she said. "It's the language of Shakespeare; people don't understand it these days."

"I take your point," said Henry Thornton. "Take your point. But couldn't we have BCP occasionally?"

"It doesn't bring the young people in," she told him. "If you want that, you'll have to go elsewhere."

Major Henry Thornton had been used to giving orders – and to receiving them. He said nothing for the moment, and bided his time.

Four days later, she took her first Sunday service. "Good morning, everyone," she began. There was a muttered response; Little Westing was not used to this. "I can't hear you," she said, rather archly. "We'll try it again. Good morning!"

"As though we were a primary school class," said Alice Thompson afterwards.

"It certainly wasn't sixth-formers she taught," said Geoffrey.

Her sermon was unexceptionable. They found later that her sermons came off the Internet.

There were storms, and lulls. The chair scheme came to nothing; there was no money for it. Anyway, it would have required a faculty. But she insisted that they buy a new hymn book, to replace their rather battered English Hymnals. The new book had most of the better hymns, but with the inner harmonies ironed out and simplified; Geoffrey played the old versions, and no one noticed. But it also contained banality, illiteracy and rubbish: *'You're my friend and you ARE my brother'*, *Shine, Jesu, Shine*, with its tired syncopations. Geoffrey played the new hymns, or 'worship songs', as they were called, through gritted teeth; Abel Trevissick didn't know them, and no one else sang much anyway.

There was trouble about her Saturdays. One Saturday morning, a recently-retired priest who sometimes took their Eucharists rang in to say he was ill. Henry Thornton, on his own initiative, contacted dear old Father Maurice, eighty if he was a day, who had seen them through their period without a priest. Henry drove him both ways and gave him lunch, so as not to deprive the church of its service – and was rebuked for it by Abigail.

"That old man's past it. You should have had a lay-led Morning Prayer."

He *was* past it, of course. During the interim, Herbert Strang, a fussy little man whom they had not seen much of lately, had also objected. But they all liked Father Maurice, and it had only been for a few months.

"That woman gets my goat," Henry muttered.

And more recently, there was the matter of Frederick. Nigel Martin, solicitor's clerk and churchwarden, was a bachelor. No one in Little Westing thought much about this, or if they did, no one commented. 'Coming out of the closet' was an urban concept; it hardly applied in a place like Little Westing. But if Nigel had wanted to come out, he could hardly have done so more obviously than by producing Frederick. Frederick worked in London – at what, no one was quite sure. To start with, he came for occasional weekends, then he began visiting more regularly; finally, he seemed to be living with Nigel. He did not always come to church, but when he did, he came exquisitely dressed: typically, a pale grey suit, pale pink shirt with a mauve tie and matching handkerchief – a sort of pastel effect – and pointed, Italian-looking black shoes. Little Westing was not a dressy place. Nigel's formal wear was subfusc; he looked like what he was, a solicitor's clerk. Henry Thornton wore shiny suits, with an old tweed coat in winter. Geoffrey himself alternated his two sports coats, with corduroy trousers when it got colder. None of the women was remotely elegant; the nearest approach was Millie's sister, who came down for a few days twice a year. Frederick stood out like an exotic. And his manners were definitely camp. His voice, his gestures, his conversation (his failed soufflé – "A *disaster*, my dears!") left no one in doubt.

Abigail, it was noticed, always greeted him rather stiffly, as though she did not know what to make of him; she had also become a little cool towards Nigel. And then one Sunday she preached a sermon, some of which was certainly not off the Internet. The Church of England was tearing itself apart over women bishops, gay bishops, gay blessings – issues which hardly touched Little Westing, who were more concerned with how to pay their parish share to the diocese, and who they could get to repair the church tower clock. But the Reverend Abigail had decided to have her say. She began with anodyne stuff about inclusivity, listening to each other, respecting each other's views, the importance of church unity. There was a little historical background: the Council of Nicaea, the Arian controversy, God working his purpose out. But then she said that the way to know God's mind was to study the Bible; the answers to all our doubts and questions lay there. It seemed an unexceptionable sentiment, but she put such stress on it that it was soon seen by the discerning for what it was: a coded message.

9

"Well," said Alice afterwards, "we know where *she* stands."

"Do we?" said Geoffrey, who had only been half listening.

"Oh, yes. That back-to-the-Bible stuff means anti-gay. She's referring to those texts in St Paul, and Leviticus, isn't it? It was aimed at Nigel and Frederick."

"St Paul also says that a woman shouldn't speak in the church."

"She's doing what they all do," said Alice. "Picking out the bits that suit herself."

"*You* speak in the church, you know," said Geoffrey; he enjoyed gently teasing Alice, who sometimes read the Lesson, as they all did.

"Yes, but I'm not a Biblical fundamentalist. That lot are more trouble than they're worth."

Henry Thornton had picked it up, too; he was sharper than he looked. "Bit of sympathy with her for once," he said. "That Frederick fellow's a regular poofter. Apologies, Alice."

"So's Nigel probably," said Alice. Nigel Martin was well out of earshot.

"Oh, Martin's all right," said Henry (who always used surnames). "Doesn't make a song and dance about it. Useful chap, anyway."

"He seems to have lost his head a bit over Frederick," said Geoffrey mildly.

"It's only like one of us falling for an unsuitable woman. Happens all the time – present company excepted, of course. I saw quite a bit of it in the army, particularly abroad. Hot climate, you know."

And he strode off down the lane with Millie, his wife of forty-odd years. Henry and Millie lived in a bungalow three or four minutes' walk away, with a long garden which stretched down the hill towards the main road. The garden was Millie's realm. She was a tall, bony, awkward woman with large hands and feet and a diffident air, as though she were trying to look smaller than she was. She lived very much in Henry's shadow;

the garden was the one place where she seemed relaxed. They were used to seeing her out in all weathers, planting, weeding, cutting back – whatever it was that gardeners did. (Geoffrey was no gardener; Margery had done all that.) She wore slacks and old shirts of Henry's in the summer, a sou'-wester and a grubby mac in winter. And gardening gloves, and gumboots. In theory, there was a church flower rota; in practice, Millie did almost all of it. Henry confined himself to mowing the lawn and trimming the hedges, with military precision.

"It's good for her," he said. "Been moving around all our life. Never had a place to call her own."

And so, sixteen months after The Reverend Abigail Lee's arrival, Geoffrey found himself walking over the wet cobbles, to a Compline whose aftermath would change their lives.

As he opened the church door, he was aware of conversation, suddenly broken off. Abigail and Nigel Martin were facing each other in front of the carved choir screen. She looked heated, but determined, as though she had been challenged and was holding her own. He seemed tense, troubled, almost upset. The usual handful of others arrived, in ones and twos. Henry was glowering and Millie looked frightened. They always sat in the chancel for Compline, in what were the old choir stalls. *"The Lord Almighty grant us a quiet night and a perfect end,"* Abigail began. Henry snorted.

Afterwards, he could not contain himself. "Do you know what that *bloody* woman's done now?" he said, as he, Geoffrey and Millie stood outside Geoffrey's small front gate. "Martin rang me from the office. Apparently he made a remark on Sunday about the difficulty of paying the parish share – and now she wants to see all the accounts for the past six months. Poor fellow's come straight from work – just gone home to get them. Not up to date, of course – end of the financial year's six months away. And that's only the half of it," he went on. "She's been snooping through the Service Register." The Service

Register, kept in the vestry, recorded all services, who took them, numbers present, numbers of communicants where relevant, and the amount of the collection. "She says we're not giving enough. Probably right. But *then*," he went on, "she more or less hinted that Martin had his hand in the till – said the collections were larger when he was away than when he wasn't." Nigel Martin, as treasurer, usually counted the money.

"Do you think that's possible?" asked Geoffrey, shocked.

"No," said Henry. "I've known some bounders in my time, a few of them very plausible. But I don't think Martin's one. He was most upset. Anyway – £20, say, out of a £70 collection? What would be the point?"

Geoffrey said nothing. Suppose Nigel Martin had a gambling habit, or was spending money on Frederick – who seemed now to be unemployed? But as Henry said, the amounts would be too small to make it likely.

"Woman's got to be stopped," said Henry. "Got to be stopped." He handed Geoffrey the church key – a regular Wednesday evening occurrence – and went off, with Millie in his wake, to their light supper. Afterwards, Geoffrey knew, he would walk across the lane to see old Bill Bowker, as he did most Wednesdays. Bill was about eighty-five, had served in the army during the war, and had spent some time as a tea-planter in India. Old Bill was not a churchgoer, but no doubt old Bill would hear all about it.

Geoffrey closed his front door and poured himself a gin and tonic. He and Margery had bought School House, where he still lived, on his retirement; it was formerly the tied dwelling of the village schoolmaster. Immediately to their left was the Village Hall, which was once the school. On the other side was the entrance to the churchyard; Geoffrey's was the nearest house to the church. Soon, he heard Nigel's car returning, and the sound of the church gate. It was a double gate, with a metal bracket at the top to keep the halves together; it warped in wet weather, and sometimes needed a kick to make it open, or a sharp tug, if you were the other side. The series of gate noises – the lifted bracket, the kick, the rattle of the bolt on the fastened side – were very familiar to Geoffrey. Half an hour or so later, he heard the gate again, and the sound of Nigel's car leaving. He wondered whether Nigel had taken the accounts with him, or whether Abigail was studying them in the church. Twenty minutes later still, while he was eating his supper, he thought he heard the gate for a third time, quieter now, as though someone were opening it carefully. Abigail departing? Though there was no sound of a car. His curtains were pulled to, and he did not look out. He put on some Mozart, and did his best to think no more about it.

An early riser, Geoffrey liked to practise the organ once a week. A brief improvisation, four hymns and a little voluntary hardly taxed him, but arthritis had crept into his fingers, and what they needed was not so much practice as exercise. Henry usually opened the church about ten o'clock, but on Wednesdays, Compline nights, he habitually gave the key to Geoffrey, so that Geoffrey could open up in his own time the next morning, save Henry the trouble, and return the key afterwards. Nigel Martin also had a key, and Abigail had insisted on one of her own.

This morning, Geoffrey was surprised to find the church unlocked. He also saw that the table lamp in the vestry, an old anglepoise, had been left on. The vestry was at the north east end of the church, behind the organ; you could enter it through a wooden door in the chancel, or through another door, part of the screen itself, at the end of the north aisle. It was a dull morning, and the spread of light from the anglepoise was visible on the wall of the vestry, above the screen. Geoffrey walked up the central aisle, turned left, looked through the tracery of the carved wooden door, and opened it. Abigail was sitting on a stool at the table, with her back to him; her head was resting on her arms. On the left side of the table was a neat pile of papers; others were covered by her head and torso. There was a large wound in her back, just below the left shoulder-blade, and a lot of blood. Geoffrey moved closer, and touched her other shoulder gently. The blood was congealed, dried, darkening. She was evidently dead.

Geoffrey remembered his mobile; Margery had insisted they each had one, in case of emergencies. He kept his charged still; though he hardly used it, it was one more way of remembering her. He stood by the church door, to keep anyone else out, and rang Henry. He was surprised at his own calmness.

Henry was there within minutes; he took in the situation at once. "Emergency services," he said. "You guard the door. I'd better ring Martin, too; he ought to know." And he stood in the churchyard to get a better signal. Another surprise was that Henry, too, had a mobile.

After that, the police took over. They sealed off the churchyard, and the church itself. A uniformed constable stood by the gate. There was much coming and going. Towards evening, a plain van drove away, evidently carrying Abigail's body. Her car, Geoffrey realised, was still parked by the village green. Geoffrey kept to his house; the news would travel fast enough without him. Anyway, he would hardly know what to say; now that he had taken it in, it was all too shocking. He needed quiet.

But the next day, Friday, he made his way across the green to the village shop, where he found Abel Trevissick holding forth; his audience was a couple of farmers' wives – not churchgoers – and Paddy, the Irish shopkeeper. Abel, as a Special Constable, was supposed to have inside knowledge about police matters – which, indeed, he did. The constable on the gate was his special friend, Alfred; 'Alfred says' was a staple of Abel's conversation.

"Alfred says they d'know the sort of knife that killed 'er,"
he was saying. "You could find'n in most kitchens. So it might
have been any one of us, m'dears," he concluded, with a look
at the women. Geoffrey supposed that it could; it was not a
comfortable thought.

After lunch, the police came to see him – a Detective Sergeant
and a Constable (not Alfred, who was in the uniformed branch).
The Detective Constable took notes. Geoffrey told them what
he knew: who was at Compline, the car arriving and leaving,
the later opening of the gate by someone on foot. He had been
in his house all evening; no, he couldn't prove it. Then he
described the discovery of the body. He was, he realised, a
potential suspect – an unfamiliar sensation. He was relieved
not to be asked about Abigail; it would have been
uncomfortable to speak ill of the so recently dead. Instead, they
asked about his movements in the church.

"When you arrived for your service – Compline, is it?" said
the Sergeant, "what route did you take to the pews you sat
in?"

"We went straight up the central aisle," Geoffrey told him.

"All of you?"

"I think so."

"And the Reverend Lee, if she went to the vestry afterwards,
which entrance would she use?"

"Almost certainly the wooden door in the chancel; it would
be the natural thing to do."

"And when you went to the church the next morning, how
did you make your way to the vestry?"

"Up the central aisle again, and turned left under the
pulpit."

"And Major Thornton the same?"

"Yes."

"So no one, as far as you know, used the north aisle leading
up to the vestry, either on Wednesday night or Thursday
morning?"

"Not as far as I know."

"Thank you, sir." And then, rather surprisingly, "Do you have a pair of gumboots, and may I see them?"

Geoffrey had never needed Wellingtons until he came to Little Westing. But he had dug their small garden for Margery at first, and later the boots had been useful for walks down muddy lanes. He had not used them for several months now.

The Detective Sergeant inspected them without comment. "Thank you, sir," he said.

About tea-time Alice Thompson, his plain-speaking friend, telephoned. "Have the police been round?" she said.

"Yes."

"Asking about gumboots?"

"Yes."

"Come to supper. I know you were only here last week, but we can talk about it. Come a bit early."

Alice had spent her youth caring for an invalid mother, and her maturer years keeping house for her late bachelor brother, a country doctor. In spite of this, her suppers were rather basic – cottage pie, sausage and mash. But he did not go to Alice's for the cooking, and – yes – it was time to talk.

She showed him into her small sitting-room – a chintz-covered three-piece suite, a book-case with old Everyman editions, little ornaments, photos of her father, mother and brother. She poured him a dry sherry; it was the only place he drank it. He always took a bottle of wine; what they left would last Alice for a week. "Come and sit at the table," she said. It was a gate-legged table in the window, not used for eating; they would eat in the kitchen later.

On the table was a large sheet of paper divided into three columns, headed 'Suspects', 'Motive' and 'Opportunity'. "Now," she said, "who do you think might have done it?"

"Alice…" said Geoffrey. "Ought we to be doing this? The poor woman's only been dead for two days."

"Think of it as a game," said Alice, "an exercise."

"Well…" said Geoffrey. "A criminal lunatic."

Alice wrote 'Criminal Lunatic' in the 'Suspects' column.

"And a lunatic doesn't need a motive," Geoffrey went on. 'N/A', wrote Alice, for 'Not Applicable', under 'Motive'.

"And as to opportunity, any time after Nigel left." A tick under 'Opportunity'.

"Go on," said Alice.

"A revengeful figure from her past," said Geoffrey. "There could have been several of those."

'Revengeful Figure from the Past', wrote Alice, with a tick in the 'Motive' column. "The difficulty's the opportunity," she said. "It was there, but how would an outsider know about it?" She put a large question mark under 'Opportunity'. "Go on," she said.

Geoffrey knew what she was after; he had been stalling. "You want me to name names," he said. "Alice, we're talking about our friends."

"It could have *been* one of our friends," she said, with a direct look. "Anyway, as I said, it's just an exercise."

"Well, just as an exercise – Henry," said Geoffrey. "The last thing we heard him say was something like 'The woman's got to be stopped'. He was getting to the end of his tether. Not that it's a motive for murder, exactly. Old Henry?"

Alice ignored the last bit. 'Henry', she wrote in the 'Suspects' column, with a large tick under 'Motive'. "The difficulty's the opportunity again," she said. "Henry goes to see Bill Bowker on Wednesdays – eight-thirty till ten, regular as clockwork. Millie told me."

"I don't think he could have done it *before* eight-thirty," said Geoffrey. "And he wouldn't expect Abigail to stay as late as ten o'clock." And then he remembered something. On a restless, hot evening last July, a Wednesday, he had taken a stroll down the lane after supper. Just outside Bill Bowker's front porch was Henry, smoking a pipe. Geoffrey had greeted him.

"Always like a pipe about nine," Henry had said. "Old Bill doesn't, though. Bad for his lungs."

Geoffrey told Alice.

"How long does it take to smoke a pipe?" she said. "Ten minutes? Three minutes up to the church, three minutes back, four minutes to – " She put a tick in the 'Opportunity' column.

"Provided Bill didn't see him go," said Geoffrey.

"Bill's sitting-room's at the back," said Alice. "Who else?"

"Nigel," said Geoffrey. "He could have killed her before he left, in which case my second person arriving is a problem; or he could have gone home by car and come back on foot, in which case the second person is Nigel himself."

"And she'd just accused him of fiddling the books."

"Well, stealing from the collection, actually, but no doubt she was working up to it. So either he *had* been fiddling, and was trying to cover it up, or he hadn't, and he was outraged."

"How would he cover it up?" said Alice.

"There were a lot of papers on the table," said Geoffrey, "but we don't know that all of them were there. He could have removed some."

"I don't suppose he'd have shown her the compromising ones in the first place," said Alice. Nevertheless, she put a large tick under both 'Motive' and 'Opportunity'. "And there was another motive," she said, "the anti-gay sermon." And a second tick went under 'Motive'. "Which would give Frederick a motive, too."

"Frederick goes to bingo in town on Wednesdays," said Geoffrey.

"So *he* says," said Alice.

None of them ever quite knew what to talk about to Frederick, but bingo was always a standby. "How was the bingo, Frederick?" "*Wonderful,* my dears – me, and all those old *trouts.* I won fifteen pounds." It was curious, thought Geoffrey, how Abel Trevissick's dialect 'm'dear' and Frederick's 'my dears' had such different effect.

Alice added Frederick's name to the list, with a tick and a question mark.

"And now," she said with a twinkle, "what about you? Living where you are, you had the best opportunity of the lot – and you could make up any stories you liked about the gate. And as to motive, there are all those awful hymns you complain about."

"Have you ever known murder done for the sake of hymnody?"

"There's always a first time."

"Well, if you're putting me down, you'll have to put in Abel, too. You know what she thought of his plainsong."

"Abel lives with his sister. He's probably got an alibi."

"Probably. And I've known opera singers with the temperament for a dozen murders," said Geoffrey. "But none of them was much like Abel."

Nevertheless, she wrote down both Abel and Geoffrey, with a question mark under Abel's opportunity.

There was a pause.

"We're forgetting Herbert," said Geoffrey.

"So we are."

It was easy to forget Herbert Strang; they had seen little of him lately (he had not been to Compline), and he was, in any case, not held in very high regard. If Nigel Martin was carefully courteous, Herbert Strang was positively tight – a fussy, pedantic little man whose formality verged on the ridiculous. He was about fifty, an accountant in a small way. He had short grey hair which stood up like a brush, and a little, clipped moustache. He wore suits with waistcoats; the jackets, which he buttoned, always looked too tight, and the arms too short. He wore brown boots. He came from a Methodist background; it was he who had objected to poor old Father Maurice, on the grounds that 'the people were not being taught'. He was right, of course. Father Maurice's sermons rambled, in general direction and in detail; sentences started well enough, only to

19

run themselves into the sand. But everyone liked old Maurice, it was only for a few months, as Henry said – and Herbert had been choked off.

Herbert himself was training to be a Lay Reader. His own addresses were of the low church sort that plod through every verse of each reading, telling you what you could easily see for yourself. His training, blessedly, had made him more concise, but had also encouraged him to begin with an amusing or relevant anecdote; these always fell flat.

A year ago, however, Geoffrey and Alice had heard something rather surprising. Abigail Lee had lived at Hanbrooke, in the vicarage attached to the largest of her six churches. Her mother lived with her. One Sunday morning, the congregations of all her churches had gone to Hanbrooke for a joint service; afterwards, there were to be drinks at The Grange. The Grange was a large Georgian house with extensive grounds, which were opened once a year for charity. It was owned by the FitzAlans, a pleasant, hearty couple in their fifties, who behaved a little like the Lord and Lady of the Manor, but were very good to the church. Geoffrey had not been into the house before.

There were two high-ceilinged living rooms, with slightly shabby furniture, some of it antique. One room held a baby grand, covered with a velvet cloth and spread with canapés. The other had a whole wall of books: Jane Austen, Dickens, Trollope's *Barchester* novels, Geoffrey noticed, but also more obviously 'churchy' authors – Charlotte M. Yonge, Barbara Pym. And books on music: a Brahms biography, the Britten letters. He was not quite sure what he had been expecting: *Country Life*, perhaps, and *The Shooting Times*.

After a while, Geoffrey found himself standing next to Alice (to whom he had given a lift) and Abigail's mother, a thin, bird-like little woman, who twittered. She was being offered another glass of wine.

"Oh, really, I *mustn't*," she was saying. "I shan't be in

command of my faculties. Oh, all right, then" – with the look of a naughty schoolgirl – "*perhaps* I will." Her cheekbones were flushed; she was obviously unused to alcohol.

"I expect Abigail's been stirring you up," she said brightly. "She gave her last parish *quite* a shake. *Such* a lot of old fuddy-duddies. But some of them approved of her in the end. She's always been very popular, you know." Alice gave Geoffrey a look; this seemed to be almost a *non sequitur*. "She had *several* proposals of marriage when she was younger," the little woman went on, "but she turned them all down. None of them was good enough for her. And it's the *funniest* thing," she continued, "but we think we recognised one of her old beaux in your congregation. Oh!" she interrupted herself, with an exaggerated double take. "I think I'm telling tales out of school. *Well,*" in a conspiratorial whisper, "actually, it was your Herbert Strang. *Such* an absurd young man. I'm afraid she thought him rather a joke. We certainly didn't see much of him after that. But you *mustn't* tell Abigail I told you."

Geoffrey and Alice decided to tell no one; if Abigail's mother chose to broadcast it, that was her affair.

Poor Herbert, thought Geoffrey afterwards, brought face to face, after all these years, with that humiliating ghost from the past. And he noticed in the months that followed that Herbert avoided Abigail. She took three of their four services a month, occasionally only two. Herbert was usually present when she was not; when she *was* there, he was often 'on a course', or observing in other churches, or sometimes, as a probationary Lay Reader, taking their services. And he had resigned from the Parish Church Council. "I have so little time," he had said. "I have all these essays to write, such a lot of research."

Yes, they had forgotten Herbert Strang. Though he was earnest enough about his religion, it was difficult to take him seriously.

Alice was completing her list. "So there's your Revengeful

Figure from the Past," she said, and wrote in Herbert's name, with a large tick under 'Motive'.

"Opportunity?" said Geofrey.

"We don't know," and she added a question mark.

"And why wait sixteen months?"

"Perhaps she's just laughed at him *again*," said Alice, and she went out to the kitchen to grill sausages.

On the following day, the Saturday, two things happened, one much more startling than the other. The first was the departure of Frederick. Geoffrey spotted his open-topped sports car speeding past the green and down the lane to the main road; it was nine o'clock in the morning. Frederick did not return Geoffrey's wave.

Later, Geoffrey went to the village shop for milk, and found Abel Trevissick telling Paddy about it. (Abel's police titbits, he was to discover, were highly unprofessional.) "Didn't have no alibi," Abel was saying. "Alfred don' know where he was, but he weren't at bingo. They'm not seen him there for weeks. Mr. Martin thrown him out, I reckon."

A lover's quarrel, thought Geoffrey; Frederick two-timing Nigel, perhaps. He remembered Henry's remark about the male equivalent of 'an unsuitable woman'. I must tell Alice, he thought, when I next see her.

And then in the evening came the news that shook the village: Henry Thornton had been taken in for questioning. He had not been charged; he was 'helping the police with their enquiries'. Bill Bowker had seen the police car drawing away.

Alice telephoned. "It must have been the gumboots," she said. "You know those questions about the aisle we used at Compline? We all walked up the central aisle, of course. They must have found a footprint from Henry's gumboot, in the north aisle. It had been wet earlier, you remember."

Most people's gumboots were black, or green; Henry's were

khaki, Geoffrey recalled. Old army issue? A different pattern, perhaps, an unusual footprint.

"I can hardly believe it, though" said Geoffrey. "Henry!"

"Nor can I," said Alice. Her lists, clearly, were one thing; faced with reality, she took a different line. "I've been in to see Millie," she went on.

"How is she?"

"She doesn't want anyone with her; she'd rather be alone. She looks terrible."

It weighed on Geoffrey's mind for the rest of the evening. He thought he knew Henry, though they were hardly intimates. But how well did you know anyone, if you had not met till you were both retired? Old Henry, though... He went to bed troubled.

There was no service at Little Westing on the Sunday; it had been decided to hold a joint service at Hanbrooke, the largest church in their group. The usual Little Westing faces were there, all except Millie – and Henry, of course. It was understood that Millie's sister was coming to stay. The Hanbrooke congregation were known for their welcome, but today, Geoffrey noticed, they were not only solemn but wary, as though questions might be intrusive, but beyond that they hardly knew what to say.

The Archdeacon took the service, and also preached. His text was '*In the midst of life, we are in death*'. He paid tribute to the dead woman – her enthusiasm, the vigorous nature of her ministry, her desire that the church should not stand still. The killer, he said, had drawn a line through all that. But God had drawn another line, a circle, surrounding her, and the murderer, with his divine love.

But just before the end there was a curious passage, saying – what, exactly? It began by considering how we ought all to react, but went on, through phrases like 'decent reticence' and 'private matters', to what seemed like an admonition not to talk to the press. Geoffrey suspected the Bishop's hand in this;

the Bishop had a reputation as a politician, a sweeper of things under carpets. Whether or not the papers seized on such stories seemed to Geoffrey to be more or less random; so far, they had shown only a mild interest. Clearly, though, from the Bishop's point of view (and that of the Church as a whole, Geoffrey realised), the less sensation the better.

For several days, the village was in shock. There was much to discuss, but little new to say. The inquest, which Geoffrey had to attend, had added nothing to what they knew already. He did not contact Alice, nor she him. Something was nagging at him, though, and he would have talk to her soon.

Abigail's funeral, at Hanbrooke, was on the following Friday. Though it was a working day, there was a decent turnout – respect for the office, more than the woman, he thought. Abigail's mother was the chief mourner. She was bowed, and looked thinner than ever as she followed the coffin to the graveside. He could not see her face under the thick veil. She was a silly woman, he knew, but grief was lending her dignity. She, at least, had loved Abigail; it was what mothers were for.

"Millie's sister's had to go home," said Alice, as he drove her back to Little Westing. Millie's sister was married to a retired merchant banker; he was in the early stages of Parkinson's, and could not be left for long. "I'll go and see Millie later."

"Come and have tea afterwards," said Geoffrey. "There's something I want to say to you."

She came about five o'clock; she was looking thoughtful.

"It's Millie," she said. "It's all rather odd."

Geoffrey made tea, and found some shortbread biscuits.

"But you go first," she said, when they were settled. "I'll tell you about Millie in a minute."

"Well," said Geoffrey, "it's little things. The final opening of the gate on the night of the murder, which if the police are right must have been Henry, was quiet, almost furtive. Nigel leaving was very much louder. Henry doesn't do furtive."

"He might if he were about to do murder," said Alice. "And Nigel was probably overwrought."

"All right. Well then, whoever killed Abigail left the vestry light on. You know what a stickler Henry is about such things – switching off lights, not turning the heaters on too soon, anything to save twopence. It isn't like him."

"Fingerprints?" said Alice.

"Perhaps. He could have worn gloves. But then – there's the gumboots. We all know about their shoe fetish, of course." Henry's shoe fetish was an insistence that no outdoor shoes should cross his threshold. Henry indoors wore rather superior leather bedroom slippers; Millie had some shabby fluffy things. "Why gumboots?" Geoffrey went on. "He was only walking a few yards across the lane to Bill's. Bill isn't too fussy about his carpets – but Henry could hardly have sat in gumboots in Bill's living room. He'd have worn his usual brown brogues. And there'd have been no sense in going back to his own house for gumboots. It doesn't fit."

"Mm… I'll tell you about Millie," Alice said. "She was distressed when I went in. Almost the first thing she said was 'Henry's so noble. I don't know what to do'. 'What do mean?' I said. Then she said she was utterly ignorant about bank accounts, and servicing the car, and so on; but I don't think she really meant that at all."

"'Henry's so noble…'" said Geoffrey. He considered it.

"I was at school with Millie, you know," said Alice, surprisingly.

"Good heavens! Where?"

"Cheltenham Ladies' College."

"*Miss Buss and Miss Beale*
Cupid's darts do not feel," Geoffrey intoned.

"*Miss Beal and Miss Buss,*
They are not like us," said Alice. "Miss Buss was North London

25

Collegiate; Miss Beale was *our* headmistress – long before my time, of course. There was a portrait of her in the hall, beside the staircase. I was told off once for sliding down the banisters."

Geoffrey tried, and failed, to imagine Alice as a schoolgirl. "What was Millie like then?" he asked.

"Oh, I hardly knew her; she was two or three years younger. She was a well-brought-up little girl, I think. But I seem to remember a temper – something about a foul and a lacrosse match. She began nurse's training afterwards, but she never finished it. Henry swept her off."

"Do you think Henry ever saw the temper?"

"Who can say? But she knew the score; she came from an army family herself. Her job was to support Henry."

She seemed to have led them down a bypath. There was a brief silence. Alice, he realised, was trying to come to a decision; and now she had made it. "I'm going see Millie again," she said. "You come, too." And she told him why.

Millie opened the door to them; she had the look of a frightened rabbit. She had obviously been crying.

"May we come in?" said Alice.

Millie showed them, unresisting, into their tidy, low-ceilinged living room. On a side-table were photos of their children and grandchildren, and a wedding picture of Henry and Millie, absurdly young. Some rather jolly cartoons of boar-hunting hung on the walls. Millie sat in her usual armchair by the fire; Geoffrey and Alice took the settee. Henry's chair they left unoccupied.

"Millie," said Alice, as soon as they had sat down, "I think you've got something to tell us." They had not discussed an approach; even for Alice, Geoffrey thought, this was pretty direct.

Millie looked startled, then appalled, then terrified; finally, her face crumpled. She put her head in her hands and sobbed; her shoulders heaved. Geoffrey could think of no way to comfort her, and Alice clearly thought comfort inappropriate. She wanted the truth.

"It was – " Millie began, trying to control herself. "Henry – " She looked up, and wiped her eyes with her hand, like a child. "Henry said we had to leave Little Westing. He said he wouldn't work with that woman any more, and we couldn't possibly stay here and *not* go to church. He said we'd have to move, to somewhere smaller; this place would get too big for us soon, anyway." She paused, and almost began sobbing again. She was a large, ungainly woman; it was, in the truest sense, pathetic. "But this – this is all I've got, all that I've ever had. The garden, the church flowers…" It was almost a wail. "And it's only because of that stupid *woman*," she went on, with a complete change of tone. It was the first flash of temper Geoffrey had seen from her. If Abigail had been Henry's long-term mistress, she could hardly have been more venomous.

"Millie, why did you wear Henry's gumboots?" Alice asked, as though continuing a quite different conversation. She did not sound hard, just curious.

"They were by the door," said Millie, not looking at them now. "Mine were filthy with mud; I'd been out in the rain. I do wear Henry's sometimes," she went on. "My feet are almost as big as his. I didn't think… And then the police came, and there were the footprints in the aisle…"

And Millie would naturally use the north aisle, thought Geoffrey, the only person who would. The church flower paraphernalia was kept at the back of the aisle, behind the last pew: pots, Oasis, the large plastic container they used for water. Millie's stuff.

"She heard me coming," said Millie, "but she never turned round. She was only going to do that when she was ready, to put me in my place. Though she can't have known it was me. And then I – " Head in her hands again, quiet now. Geoffrey remembered her nurse's training; she would have known where to put the knife in.

"Shall I ring the police, or will you?" said Alice, looking at Millie.

"But Henry decided, Henry wanted – " Millie began, her large hands fluttering. You never knew what went on in a marriage, Geoffrey thought. Henry's view of marriage was Pauline: the wife should be subservient to the husband. But he treated Millie, and indeed all women, with the greatest courtesy; beneath it, clearly, was the fixed idea that woman, as the weaker vessel, was to be protected. It was dreadful to think of his taking this to its logical conclusion, going off with the police voluntarily, knowing that Millie was guilty. Geoffrey wondered if the two of them had communicated, or whether Henry had simply taken the initiative. There would have been, at the very least, an exchange of looks.

"Henry – " Millie began again; for her, clearly, the one priority still was what Henry wanted.

"It won't do, Millie," said Alice. And she went out into the hall to telephone.

After that, things started to take their course. Millie was arrested, and Henry released. The police found the murder weapon at the bottom of the garden, buried in the potato bed. Millie's trial would not be for several months. She had entered no plea at the Magistrate's hearing, but if, as they all suspected, she were eventually to plead guilty, the trial would be a brief affair. No weeks of sensation to upset the bishop. And none of them, with luck, would be called as witnesses.

Geoffrey went to see Henry the day after his return; he was looking old, but was keeping up appearances.

"Anything I can do?"

"No thanks, old boy. Shan't be here much longer." It was difficult to know what else to say. Expressions of sympathy seemed out of order, and Henry was not the man to talk about his affairs. One did not discuss one's wife, even in these circumstances. Soon enough, they heard that he had rented a flat not far from the women's prison, to be near Millie. A 'For Sale' notice went up outside his house. He had resigned as churchwarden, with immediate effect. And so he passed out of their lives, with no farewell.

Nigel Martin tried to resign, too, but was persuaded not to for the sake of continuity. He insisted, though, on giving up his post as treasurer. They all thought this was unnecessary. His accounts, and related papers, had gone to the Diocesan Board of Finance; they were returned, with a note saying that they wished all other churches were so meticulous. As to the supposed discrepancies in the collection, these were explained by Henry, in a postscript to his resignation letter. Millie's sister, married to her merchant banker, visited twice yearly and always came to church; on the last two occasions, Nigel had been away, and Henry had counted the collection. Each time, it had contained a £20 note. Most of them paid in weekly Gift Aid envelopes; a note of that size was a rarity. It could only have been Millie's sister. Nevertheless, Nigel was insistent; the moment there was the least doubt of one's probity, he said, one could not go on. Herbert Strang took over as treasurer; within two months, he was also the second churchwarden. The posts were not supposed to be held by the same person – but who else was there? By Christmas, Herbert would have finished his Lay Reader's training. They would see a great deal more of him, with his fussy manner, his 'teaching the people'.

And life would go on, Geoffrey supposed, as it had through the Reverend Abigail Lee's excesses; it had gone on here for six hundred years. But for how much longer? The whole Anglican Communion was in crisis. There was a woman Primate in the U.S.A., gay blessings in Canada, an Archbishop breathing hate in Nigeria, lunatic Puritans in Sydney. And their own Archbishop agonising and temporising, trying to hold it together, to prevent schism. But the threat to Little Westing, and churches like them, was not any of this; it was economic. With their dwindling congregations and decreasing funds, how could they hope to keep going? The Church of England was collapsing under its own weight.

And Geoffrey realised suddenly that it was not so much the worship that he cared for as the building itself, that precious small gift on his own doorstep. All of it. The funny little organ, with the E below middle C that stuck, and the low A flat which depressed so far you had to pull your little finger back out of the hole. The carved screen, and the crude Norman font from an even earlier church. The bit of stained glass which might show Edward VI holding his new Prayer Book – or might not. The cheerful red kneelers made by ladies of the village (Alice, Margery) to celebrate the millennium. The new altar for the side chapel, hand-crafted by Abel Trevissick, and blessed by the Bishop. The building – and the community that cherished it, the two or three gathered together: Nigel Martin, conscientiously dealing with long-drawn-out grant applications, Henry saving twopence where he could, poor Millie's flowers... It could not go on much longer, here or elsewhere. But he, at least, would make a final journey over the cobbles when his time came. It would see him out.

Two

LAKE

IT WAS about a year later that the package arrived from Mick. 'Alison and I have been sorting through some of Uncle Julius's stuff,' Mick wrote. 'It's been up in the loft for most of twenty years. As you're the only one of us who reads poetry, we thought you might find it interesting.'

Mick was Geoffrey's brother-in-law. The several generations of Geoffrey's family can be simply explained. His Uncle Julius had been his mother's brother. Of his own generation, Geoffrey was the only survivor; his sister, Claire, who had been married to Mick, had died five years ago. Mick had worked for an engineering firm; though Geoffrey and he had little in common, he found Mick amiable enough, and Mick and Claire had always seemed contented. Alison, Claire and Mick's daughter, was the sole representative of the following generation; she had been married, but was now divorced. Uncle Julius had rather surprisingly left all his money to Alison – his great-niece – so that she was comfortably off. Finally, two generations down from Geoffrey, was Alison's own teenage daughter, Pippa.

Geoffrey and Claire's Uncle Julius, whose 'stuff' Mick and Alison had been sorting, had died eighteen years ago. Geoffrey had never been close to him. It was difficult to be close to Uncle Julius. He had always looked much the same to Geoffrey: tall, with iron-grey hair, a face that was more bone than flesh, and a sharp, beaky nose. He was intelligent, austere, and forbidding. He could do *The Times* crossword in fifteen minutes. For most of his working life he had taught English in the same boys' Grammar School, specialising in sixth form work. Geoffrey did not envy Julius's pupils; they would have been thoroughly taught, but he clearly regarded most of them as fools. He had been called up during the war, rising to the rank of captain; for two or three years, he was a prisoner of the Japanese. He never talked about that time. Geoffrey's mother said that it had changed him; when they were children, he had been an easy and companionable elder brother. Three years before the war he had married Matilda – Mattie – a gentle American lady, and they also had a daughter, Imogen, a year older than Geoffrey. But the marriage did not long survive the war, and Mattie went back to America. "No one could live with Julius," Geoffrey's mother said. "Mattie was frightened of him." Soon after Matttie left, she was killed in a car crash. Imogen, the daughter, aged nine, was doubly abandoned – and left alone with her austere father.

As she entered adolescence, Imogen began to have mental problems. There were psychiatrists; occasionally, she was hospitalised. Geofffey saw almost nothing of her in those years; indeed, he never knew much about her. But once, when Geoffrey was nineteen, she came to stay. His mother told him that Imogen had been very unhappy – a love affair, she suggested ('love affair' was one of his mother's phrases), and even, she hinted, though she was quite unsure of this, an abortion. Imogen needed a change, Geoffrey was told, and perhaps the two young people could spend time together.

It was not a success. Imogen clearly *was* unhappy; she was silent, pale, withdrawn. Geoffrey's parents did their best; they all went out to a restaurant, and to the theatre. But it did little to lift her mood.

As for Geoffrey, he floundered. Mental instability, love affairs, abortions (illegal then), he knew nothing of. Even normal girls he had had little enough to do with. After five years at a boys' Public School, where even to talk to a girl was a punishable offence, he had gone to Cambridge. There *were* girls in Cambridge, of course, but proportionately, far fewer than men, and Geoffrey had made little headway. He did not know the rules, how you went about it. Imogen, though only a year older, was clearly a lot further down the road to knowledge.

What Geoffrey remembered most was their walk to the shore. Geoffrey's parents' house was a mile and a half from the sea; the path became a sandy lane, went briefly through pine woods, and petered out in the sand hills, with their coarse grasses and sea-holly. After a while, Imogen sat down, and Geoffrey, not knowing what to do, sat by her. She looked so unhappy that, unexpectedly even to himself, he reached out a hand and touched hers. It was not calculated; it was instinctive, a gesture of fellow-feeling. Her reaction startled him. She drew away, not so much as though she had been stung, but as if his touch repelled her. Briefly, he saw it in her face, before she relapsed into blank misery. Geoffrey was shaken. He had never thought of himself as good-looking, and he had no idea how the opposite sex saw him. But was he really so unattractive? It was fortunate that in his last year at Cambridge he met Margery – after which things became comparatively simple. But that was later.

He could not remember seeing Imogen again. He was getting on with his life – marriage, his first teaching job. But he heard that Imogen, living with her father still, had disappeared. Uncle Julius did the proper things; he contacted the police, and several voluntary agencies. The police told him that as Imogen was not a minor, and a mental patient only voluntarily, she was free to go where she chose, though they put her on the Missing Persons Register. But she never turned up again, or made any contact. After some years she was officially declared dead. Whether Uncle Julius had continued to hope, he did not know.

Geoffrey and Margery had visited Julius occasionally, if they happened to be in his part of the country. He remained as austere as ever, with a caustic turn of phrase. But he always gave them tea, and was, as far as they could tell, glad to see them. The last time they saw him he was in hospital, slumped in a chair in a dressing gown, a pathetic, thin old man. "I think you'd better go," he said after a while. "I'm too miserable to be worth talking to." Margery got up and put an arm round him. Geoffrey held his breath; you did not put an arm round Uncle Julius. But he made no objection. Three weeks later, he was dead.

Very few of us left now, thought Geoffrey. He and Margery, to their regret, had had no children. There was just Alison, his sister Claire's daughter, and Alison's own teenage daughter, Pippa. And here was a message out of the past: two buff folders from his Uncle Julius, rescued after years in Alison's loft, and sent on by his brother-in-law because, of the four of them, he was the one who read poetry.

He opened the slimmer of the two folders. There were three sheets of paper only, two of them typed, on a machine which had seen much use, and the third handwritten. They were held together with a rusty paperclip. The first page contained a stretch of blank verse which Geoffrey recognised; it was an excerpt from Wordsworth's long, autobiographical *The Prelude*. On the second were two extracts he did not know; again, no indication of title or of author. Material for Uncle Julius's sixth form teaching? Leaving the third sheet to examine later, he laid the folder aside and opened the other.

Here, there were about thirty sheets, with two holes punched down the left hand side, and held together by those old-fashioned green tags. The title page said: *Poems: by Julius Allen.* This looked more interesting – and more surprising. Geoffrey paused for a moment, wondering what sort of poetry Julius would write. Satire, perhaps, and in some sort of mandarin idiom. Julius's standards were fastidious. Geoffrey remembered a visit with Margery, thirty years ago; a volume of Thomas Gray was on the carpet.

"Gray!" said Margery brightly. "We had to learn Gray's *Elegy* at school. I can still remember most of it." And like a schoolgirl saying a lesson, she got as far as line ten, '*The moping owl does to the moon complain'*, before her memory failed.

Uncle Julius listened without expression. "The owl," he said, "behaves in a very self-conscious fashion."

"So he does!" said Margery, delightedly. "I'd never have noticed it."

Julius's own poems, Geoffrey felt, would have to meet his own high standard; what he could not imagine was Julius opening up, giving himself away.

He was wrong. His first reaction was like that of A. E, Housman's sister, Clemence, on first reading *A Shropshire Lad.* "Alfred," she wrote, "has a heart." There were poems of love and loss, some, presumably, addressed to the American wife. There were poems about myths: Diana and Actaeon, Adam and Eve. In the latter, Adam, long banished from Paradise, experiences *'poena damni'*, the torments of the damned. Geoffrey remembered his mother telling him that Julius had once turned to Roman Catholicism, in the way that people sometimes did who wanted discipline, and certainty. It had not lasted. Then there was what Geoffrey thought of as 'the duffle coat poem': the middle-aged poet looks at a young girl in a coffee bar, recognising his rather banal lust, and understanding, too, the almost certain blankness and stupidity of the duffle-coated girl's mind. And finally, there were two rather troubling poems. In one, a man and a girl sit in a room, the lamp making a halo of her golden hair. Anyone looking in, says the poet, would see a peaceful, domestic scene, not recognising the *'monstrous infection'* that was there. The infection is not named, or even hinted at. In the other, Julius's fastidiousness slips for a moment. Two young people, going over a property they are considering, are appalled when out of a small lake, bordered by rhododendrons, there emerges a scaly and shocking monster. Again that word – monster – and again no explanation.

Geoffrey forgot his lunch; the poems were a little troubling. He turned back to the thin folder and read through the Wordsworth extract. The poet as a boy borrows – or purloins – a boat at night, and rows across the lake (Windermere, Geoffrey knew). A huge peak blocks out the stars, and its reflection seems to stride across the lake towards him, as he rows guiltily away. Afterwards, *'huge and mighty forms... moved slowly through the mind / By day, and were a trouble to my dreams'.*

Geoffrey remembered, suddenly, Uncle Julius's cottage. Geoffrey, after a term's music teaching, needed quiet; it was then that he read poetry. He had considered reading English at university, rather than music, but music was a talent, poetry merely an interest. His tastes were simple. He had his mother's *Palgrave's Golden Treasury* and a complete Shakespeare. Over the years, he added Donne and Herbert, unfashionable in Palgrave's time, and other poets unknown to Palgrave: Hardy, Kipling, Betjeman. And Housman: he had a particular affection for Housman, and at one time had read quite a lot about him.

Uncle Julius, by contrast, after thirteen weeks of teaching literature, wanted to get away from it. As well as his house in the Midlands, he had had a tiny cottage not far from Windermere, to which he escaped at the end of every term, even in the dead of winter. There had been a rowing boat, Geoffrey knew, kept in a shed by the lake. Presumably he took Imogen with him. Julius's affinity with the passage – the lake, the rowing boat – seemed obvious. Apart, that is, from the guilt.

The next sheet contained two rather more puzzling extracts, neither of which Geoffrey recognised. As with the first, there was no title or author.

Some feelings are to mortals given,
With less of earth in them than Heaven;
And if there be a human tear
From passion's dross refined and clear,
A tear so limpid and so meek
It would not stain an angel's cheek,
'Tis that which pious fathers shed
Upon a duteous daughter's head.

'Tis an awful thing
To touch such mischief as I now conceive:
So men sit shivering on the dewy bank,
And try the chill stream with their feet; once in...
How the delighted spirit pants for joy!

The first passage seemed self-regarding, not to say sentimental, if it really referred to Julius and his daughter; the second was clearly about temptation, though the nature of it was not named. Nor could he see how the passages were related. He put them aside to think about later, and turned to the final page – and it was about this point that he began to feel uncomfortable. Geoffrey liked patterns. He had enjoyed writing academic fugues for his degree. It was not real music, but there was something satisfying about slotting it all together: subject and counter-subject, inversion, augmentation, stretto... He had known that Henry Thornton could not be a murderer, because pieces of the pattern would not fit. Now, in these extracts, he sensed the creeping of another pattern, one he could not put a finger on yet. But if he felt chilled, it was not only because he had forgotten his lunch.

There were seven items, almost like random jottings, except that they were in Uncle Julius's careful italic script:

And through their reins in ice and fire
Fear contended with desire.

Grief fills the room up of my absent child.

Poor inch of nature.

But how oddly will it sound that I
Must ask my child's forgiveness.

And my ending is despair
Unless I be relieved by prayer.

Too much of water hast thou, poor Ophelia.

I found a thing to do.

The first, he knew, was from *A Shropshire Lad*. Housman had claimed the poem was about adultery; but Housman, as was now well known, was a severely repressed homosexual, and adultery would be the last thing on his mind.

'*Grief fills the room up of my absent child*' was from *King John*, a play he had neither seen nor read, but he recognised the line from a little Shakespeare anthology which Margery had given him. Constance was grieving for her dead child; any meaning it might have had for Julius, though, was vitiated by the fact that it was a male child.

'*Poor inch of nature*' he did not recognise. But the next two were both from *The Tempest*, a play he knew well since he had done the music for it in a school production. The first was Alonso – though again, asking forgiveness of his son, surely? And then Prospero, from the Epilogue: '*And my ending is despair...*' Hope, he thought he remembered, was a theological virtue for Roman Catholics, and despair was its opposite. But why, for Julius, despair? '*Too much of water*' was drowned Ophelia in *Hamlet*. Again, why?

It was with the last item, '*I found a thing to do*', that he began to understand what he might be looking at. He did not immediately recognise it; but he was sure that it was one of those statements like *'Something understood'* at the end of George Herbert's *Prayer*, or *'It was, you may say, satisfactory'* in Eliot's *Journey of the Magi* – a deceptively simple phrase, carrying more weight than it ought to be able to bear. Then he got it; it was Browning's *Porphyria's Lover*. The *persona* of the poem, conducting an illicit affair, strangles his lover with her own hair as her head lies on his shoulder. This was the 'thing' he had found to do.

The pattern that Geoffrey was beginning to see frightened him; but he would have to be certain. One or two pieces (Constance, Alonso) did not quite fit, and he would need the source of the three extracts he didn't recognise. The next day he wrote to Patrick Byrne, an old teaching colleague, retired like himself, but previously Head of English at his last school. They were still on Christmas card terms – and Pat enjoyed this sort of puzzle.

The reply came back within a week. 'I cheated,' wrote Pat. 'There's a thing called Google.' *'Poor inch of nature'* was from Shakespeare's *Pericles*, Act III, scene iii – another play which Geoffrey did not know. That evening, he read *Pericles*; its opening startled him, but did not (in another sense) surprise him. *'Poor inch of nature'*, from later in the play, is addressed by Pericles to his new-born daughter; they are on a boat, in a storm. The phrase was not in Geoffrey's old Bodley Head edition, but was generally accepted these days (Pat told him) as belonging there. Trust Uncle Julius, he thought, to include a textual crux.

'Some feelings are to mortals given', etc., came from Scott's narrative poem, *The Lady of the Lake*, which Geoffrey read two days later; Alice, rather surprisingly, had a copy. It was a tale set in mediaeval Scotland: a wronged father with a beautiful daughter, living in obscurity, a wicked villain who turns good in the end, a noble hero in disguise... and an inevitable happy ending. It was about as cardboard as the Wordsworth passage was real. The excerpt was what it purported to be; it described

the holiness of a father's tears over the head of his duteous daughter.

Pat had told him, too, about the other extract on the same page. It took a month for the Library Loan service to find him the complete work. And when he had read it, he was certain.

The sheets of extracts were not randomly put together by Alison and Mick. The rusty paperclip told him that; there was ancient rust on the first and third sheet. Nor were the extracts themselves random; they were a series of clues, compiled by Julius's crossword-puzzle mind. For it was clear to Geoffrey that there were two, possibly three, crimes here. To begin with, Julius had had sexual relations with his daughter, probably over years. There were hints in Julius's own poems, once you knew what you were looking at. Diana and Actaeon: the viewing of a forbidden nakedness, and the punishment of it. The duffle-coat poem, combining a rather sad (and not uncommon) middle-aged lust with a total lack of respect for the object of it. Possibly the longing for the loved one's return was for Imogen, not Mattie. But most of all, the two 'monster' poems: the peaceful, lamplit room with the *'monstrous infection'* that no onlooker would suspect, and the much more physical monster emerging from the previously untroubled lake. The monster was incest. He knew as soon as he had read Pat's letter; but he had guessed before.

For the third extract he had sent Pat was from Shelley's verse play, *The Cenci*. It tells of a late sixteenth-century Roman, Francesco Cenci, who, after a lifetime of wickedness and depravity, decides to rape his own daughter, Beatrice. The passage (*'So men sit shivering on the dewy bank / And try the chill stream with their feet; once in… How the delighted spirit pants for joy!'*) was his anticipation of the act. Housman's *Shropshire Lad* couplet (*'fear contended with desire'*) described a similar mental state, though it was not incest that was contemplated. But there *was* incest in the very first scene of *Pericles* – another father and daughter (not Pericles himself).

Geoffrey understood at last his teenage walk to the shore with Imogen, her repulsion when he reached out his hand and touched her. Poor girl, it was not personal; she would have been repelled by any man. Her father had spoilt all that for her.

And there was worse. For it now seemed clear to Geoffrey that Imogen had not just 'disappeared'; Julius had killed her, and her body was in Lake Windermere. '*I found a thing to do*': the murder of an illicit lover. The Wordsworth passage: rowing guiltily over the lake ('*with trembling oars I turned*'), and the '*huge and mighty forms*' that were '*a trouble to my dreams*'. Then there was '*Too much of water hast thou, poor Ophelia*' – a reference to the dead girl's body. And Julius's own 'lake' poem: the symbolic monster in the lake had a range of meaning, if one thought of Julius's own daughter. (And without it, the poem was both melodramatic and pointless.) More peripherally, there were fathers and daughters in boats: Prospero and the child Miranda escaping from Milan, Pericles and the infant Marina. And the Scott passage: Geoffrey appreciated now Julius's grim irony in placing the noble father's cloying devotion ('*from passion's dross refined and clear*') next to the dreadful, incestuous Count Cenci. And Scott's title itself was suggestive: Geoffrey was fairly sure that Julius, in his own mind, had thought of his dead daughter as 'The Lady of the Lake'.

Finally, there was the guilt apparent in the two *Tempest* passages. Geoffrey had assumed, wrongly, that the 'child' whose forgiveness Alonso was asking was his son, Ferdinand; but no, it was Miranda, his 'child' in the sense that she and Ferdinand were betrothed. Asking forgiveness from a girl-child: it made sense now. '*And my ending is despair / Unless I be relieved by prayer*' would be from Julius's Roman Catholic period. It tied up with '*poena damni*' in his Adam and Eve poem: the phrase (Geoffrey had looked it up) defined for Catholics the loss of the love of God, and the impossibility of ever regaining it.

He was a little less certain about the third crime, but he thought he knew, too, that Julius had made his daughter pregnant, possibly more than once, and that she had had an abortion. He remembered his mother hinting at such a thing (though she would not, of course, have guessed the father). But the indications were there. Count Cenci had gloated over the possibility of having a child by his daughter. And there were two further, suggestive, quotations. *'Poor inch of nature'* sounded like Shakespeare, to Geoffrey's musician's ear, but mathematically, it was inexact; it fitted a foetus better than a new-born babe. And Constance's lament (*'Grief fills the room up of my absent child'*) was for a boy; it did not work as a lament for Imogen. Suppose that the aborted foetus had been recognisably male, and that it was *this* child, the son whom Julius had never had, for whom he was grieving?

A second pregnancy, too, could be a motive for murder. Of course it might just have been that Imogen, aged twenty-six, no longer suited Julius's peculiar tastes. But suppose that, cowed all her life, she had at last turned on him – refusing another abortion, threatening to name the father?

Geoffrey had more than once tried to picture what had happened next. The murder done in the cottage, he thought; Porphyria was strangled by her lover in a cottage. (And on a stormy night: a wind which *'did its worst to vex the lake'*.) The body bundled into the car, transferred to the little boat (and weighted, probably – Windermere was not deep), the boat run out of the shed, rowed to the centre... The mere practicalities would have defeated Geoffrey. But he was fairly sure that Julius had done it.

The intriguing question, though, was why Julius had left the clues behind him. Geoffrey thought he knew why; it came from his knowledge of A. E. Housman. Housman, a severely repressed homosexual, had defended his private life behind an impenetrable wall. Nevertheless, he had left unpublished poems for his brother Laurence to edit after his death, which made his true position clearer. Why? Because, it seemed – in spite of his habitual reticence – that a part of him wanted it known. Housman's unrequited devotion to Moses Jackson (straight, married) was lifelong; his bequest to Laurence was a version of the lover, even the illicit lover, who feels the need to proclaim his love from the rooftops – at whatever cost to himself. And Julius's was a twisted version of the same thing.

But what now, thought Geoffrey? He could not go to the police with a bundle of poems and ask them to drag Lake Windermere – even if such a thing were possible. And had it been, it would be too late to tell whether poor Imogen was pregnant. Besides, the culprit was almost twenty years dead.

He could not, either, bring himself to tell his friend Alice. She would not be shocked, or not in an old-maidish way; she had too much sense for that. But their previous investigation had been joint, from the start; she knew nothing of this one. It was, in any case, a family matter, hardly for the world at large.

Not that there was much family. Mick was only family-by-marriage. There was just Alison, his niece, and her teenage daughter, his great-niece Pippa. He had already decided to leave what he had to Pippa; student debt, house prices – it would give her a start. He was glad, now, that he had thought of it. For he realised that he could never tell Alison what he knew. She had been left comfortably off by Julius, her great-uncle, but to tell her now would taint her comfort permanently, particularly as she had been a young girl herself when she inherited. Better to leave her in peace. And perhaps his legacy to his own great-niece, in some way not quite clear to him, would remove the taint from that earlier inheritance.

He would tell no one. But he would not destroy the evidence. He would do as Julius had done, and leave the folders to be found after his death. Perhaps someone else would come to the same conclusions. Though probably they wouldn't.

Three

THE LETTERS

IT WAS two and a half years later, and Geoffrey had grown old. A sort of weariness had crept up on him, a loss of interest. Newspapers bored him – same old stories, different names. He had stopped reading about education years ago. Even music had lost its hold; it was either over-familiar, or else new, and an effort. To weariness was added breathlessness – and then he had his 'funny turn', and was sent to hospital. Heart, he was told; he would have to take things gently. He hardly needed telling; he did not feel like doing anything else. The pills made him drowsy in the mornings.

Alice was good to him at that time. For a while she brought up food every day, or cooked for him in his own kitchen. She did bits of shopping when she went on the weekly bus to town. It was less necessary now, but she still came up with a wedge of sponge cake or a simple casserole, and tried to interest him in village affairs. She was a good neighbour.

It was after his spell in hospital that he gave up the organ. His last active music-making: it ought to have been a wrench, but somehow it wasn't. They found a lady living outside the village – Mavis Bannerman, about forty-five, divorced. She had a large, fleshy face that was all powder and lipstick, not what Geoffrey thought of as a 'real' face. There was too much flesh on her altogether. She wore smart suits, and rings; she was blonde. Alice said she had her hair done every week. Herbert Strang seemed taken with her for a while, but she soon choked him off. She liked to be noticed, though, both for herself and her performance, which was approximate. "Very nice," Geoffrey had taken to saying. It was easy to say.

They had a new team vicar, too, the Reverend Septimus Hill, aged about sixty – a tall, thin man with sparse grey hair. He had spent much of his working life in Africa, and his distant manner suggested that a part of him was still there. He did not like driving down narrow lanes, especially in the dark, and never took their occasional Evensongs. Sometimes, he forgot their names. But he did not interfere, for which they were grateful.

There was only one other new face in the congregation: John Pennington, a recently retired art lecturer. He was loose-limbed and gangling, and wore floppy sweaters, even in church. He did abstracts based on rock shapes, and sometimes, for a fee, portraits; Mavis Bannerman was known to have commissioned one. Alice had suggested that Geoffrey had his done; she thought it might interest him. But why should he want to look at his own face? He saw it every morning: the receding hair, the white beard, the deep grooves between nose and cheekbone, the scrawny neck. Anyway, he did not much like John Pennington. Pennington was left wing. His preferred newspaper was *The Guardian*, to which he sometimes wrote pithy letters. But he also took *The Telegraph*, 'to keep an eye on the Tories', and occasionally a tabloid. He spoke with a drawl and a hint of mockery; coming from the metropolis, he clearly saw them all as rustics – even Geoffrey, who was a Cambridge graduate. But then Pennington had been in Further Education; Geoffrey was a mere schoolmaster, and long-retired at that.

There were no other changes. Herbert and Nigel Martin were still churchwardens, though Nigel ought to retire soon, as five years was the recommended maximum. Nigel was a little greyer; Herbert, born middle-aged, looked much the same. As a Lay Reader, he took most of their lay-led services, continuing to preach his earnest sermons. It was Lent, and he had been telling them about sin. It was a time for self-examination, he insisted, for searching our consciences, reforming our lives. One week he touched on Original Sin, and Alice challenged him.

"You can't tell me that a *new-born baby's* sinful," she said. "It's perfectly ludicrous." Herbert looked put out; he knew what his training had told him, and he was not equipped to deal with argument. The next week, he returned to it, at greater length. "Having the last word," as Alice put it. He meant well, but it was still hard to take him seriously.

It was about this time that the letters began to arrive. The first one Geoffrey saw was to himself. It was the standard Anonymous Letter of detective fiction: words and parts of words cut from newsprint, pasted onto a sheet of white paper. The address, word-processed, and the postmark – the county town – gave nothing away. *'A FANCY WOMAN AT YOUR AGE?'* the letter said; *'DISGRACEFUL'.* 'Disgrace' and 'ful' were in different fonts, the question mark was carefully cut round. He stared at it. It could only mean Alice, which was ridiculous – at their age. He examined his conscience, as Herbert had bidden them. Alice was a friend, someone to talk to in his loneliness, but they were not intimates, even in conversation. As to anything else, he could honestly say that there was not a spark, nor could he imagine one had they been fifty years younger. He ought to be angry, he realised, but he hadn't the energy. He decided not to show it to Alice. He put it under some papers on his desk; it was less effort than anything else he could think of.

But he was outflanked by Alice; she came up at teatime. Her scraped-back hair, grey when he first knew her, was quite white now, and her plain, slightly weather-beaten face, and particularly her hands, were more wrinkled than ever. But she still stood straight-backed and said what she thought.

"You'd better see this," she said, opening her handbag and producing a piece of paper. The words were of different shapes and sizes, but the message was identical, except that 'woman' had been replaced by 'man'.

He showed her his own letter. "What ought we to do?" he said.

"Nothing," said Alice. "We can't run our lives round this sort of thing." She did not seem in the least embarrassed.

"Who do you think might have sent it?"

"I'm not going to waste my time thinking about it."

And Geoffrey decided to do the same.

Two days later, a Saturday, Geoffrey walked across to the village shop. Abel Trevissick was there – Cornishman, carpenter, Special Constable. He would do any job, large or small – fitted kitchens, patio doors, replacing a bit of damp window sill for Alice, working in his slow, methodical way, with plenty of time for tea breaks and a chat. His figure, always comfortable, was spreading; his belly hung over his broad leather belt. Not beer, people said, so much as his sister's cooking; it was all pasties and baked potatoes, and clotted cream with their scones.

Abel was showing a sheet of paper to Paddy, the Irish shopkeeper. "See this'n," he said. Geoffrey peered over Paddy's shoulder, easy to do as Paddy was so short. It was a letter like his and Alice's. *LOOK AT YOURSELF!* it read. *GREEDY PIG'*.

"I do be putting it on a bit," said Abel. "But there bain't no call for *that*."

Abel brought the letter to church next day, and showed it to anyone who had not seen it, including the team vicar, the Reverend Septimus Hill.

"That's odd," he said, in his distracted way. "I had one like that yesterday – cut-out words, and so on. It seemed to suggest that I should come here more often. Perhaps I should. I'll try to fit it in, when the weather improves." And he wandered off to drive to his next service.

That's four, thought Geoffrey: three members of the congregation, and Septimus. And possibly more that we don't know about. Soon enough, there was a fifth. Ralph and Celia Boynton, like John Pennington, were new to the village; they had bought The Old Bakery a year ago. They were middle-aged; it was a second marriage for both of them. They obviously had money; they dressed as though they were going to a county show. She was small, dark and sharp-featured; he was taller, with wavy grey hair and film-star good looks. They were not churchgoers. The Old Bakery, neglected for years, was soon transformed; they rethatched, redecorated inside and out, cut back and replanted the overgrown garden, replaced the rotting front gate. Then, unfortunately, they added a Sky TV dish. The Old Bakery was not only Grade II listed, it was also in a Conservation Area. The Planning Authority, acting on a tip-off, came round to inspect – and ordered them to remove it. They were known to be furious.

And now they, too, had received a letter. Celia Boynton had told old Paddy about it, and anyone else who would listen. "What sort of a village *is* this?" she said. "We come here, we smarten up the house which had been an eyesore for years, we employ local builders and thatchers, we spend money at the Fete, and so on – and now this." The letter said *'ANGRY? TRY OBEYING THE RULES'*.

Geoffrey soon heard about it; news travels fast in villages. And this time he did not so much feel the stirring of a pattern as see, with sudden clarity, the pattern of which the letter was a part. He would have to tell Alice, he realised. But the thought made him weary, so he did nothing for the moment.

The following Sunday, Herbert Strang took the service. We are a broken people, he assured them, and dwelt on the Pharisee and the publican. Over coffee afterwards, talk turned to the letters. Those to Abel, Septimus Hill and the

Boyntons were public knowledge; no one knew about Geoffrey's and Alice's.

"It's disgraceful!" said Herbert, and then, it seemed to Geoffrey, looked slightly sheepish, as though he wished he hadn't spoken. Most of them, in truth, were more bemused than upset, though it still gave them plenty to talk about. All except Mavis Bannerman, Geoffrey noticed; usually so voluble, on this occasion she was strangely quiet.

"There's no art to find the mind's construction in the face," said John Pennington, "or so we're told on good authority. We portrait painters think there is, of course."

"Dear me!" said Mavis, speaking for the first time. "Do you mean you can discover our guilty secrets, just by looking at us?" Pennington, they knew, had yet to start her portrait.

"I was about to add," said Pennington, "that I'm not sure it runs to spotting poison-pens."

"Three," said someone. "One wonders who'll be the next."

"There have been more than three," said Nigel Martin, a little tightly. No one challenged this; there was a certain aloofness about Nigel which did not invite it. But how did Nigel know, Geoffrey wondered. Perhaps Nigel had received one himself, in which case... in which case Geoffrey knew what it was about. Alert now, he thought he had seen all of it; the last few minutes had told him. Herbert, Mavis's silence and her remark to John Pennington, Pennington himself, Nigel, the call to the planning people... He had not a scrap of evidence, but he knew in his bones he was right. He sighed. He *would* have to talk to Alice.

She came to tea and he told her. There would be at most one more letter, he said. He told her how he knew. He also told her who was sending them.

"It's been stupid stuff," she said. "Still, even one more's too many; it ought to be stopped. We must *do* something." She was of the breed who always thought you could do something. He watched her as she busied herself about it. He wasn't sure she was acting wisely, but it was easier to let her than to argue with her.

The next thing that happened was that Herbert Strang was rushed to hospital; this was on the Wednesday. He was not at Compline. Herbert's house was part of a small stone terrace just outside the village; his office was a mile and a half further on. Neighbours had noticed his curtains drawn across, his car still parked in the road. At 11 a.m., they knocked; receiving no reply, they called the police. But by Friday, Herbert was back at work.

"It was the oddest thing," he said to them all on Sunday. "I couldn't seem to wake up somehow. They did tests, but they couldn't find anything." The others listened, with conflicting emotions. For rumour had been spreading a different tale: that Herbert Strang had taken an overdose.

Geoffrey and Alice had heard it the day before; Alice, in particular, was shocked. "We shall have to talk to Nigel," Geoffrey told her. "We probably should have done so earlier." So Nigel had been asked for drinks after Matins, with an indication that there was something to say. What did Nigel drink, Geoffrey wondered. He liked Nigel, but they were not on visiting terms. Red or white wine, he decided, or the gin and tonic which he drank himself.

He showed them into his small living room. They were a little constrained; it was a new social experience for the three of them. Alice, in particular, was silent. When Geoffrey had poured, he handed Nigel his letter. Alice had destroyed hers, but he described it.

"It was the Seven Deadly Sins, you see," he told Nigel. "I saw that first of all. Alice and I were Lust, God help us." Nigel's correct face did not alter. "Poor old Abel was Gluttony, Septimus Hill was Sloth."

"Then I was Covetousnes," said Nigel quietly.

"I was afraid of that," said Geoffrey. The old charge of

stealing from the collection. "I'm sure Mavis Bannerman had one, too, though she never said so. She kept very quiet, you remember, when we were talking about it."

"Yes," said Nigel, "I noticed that,"

"I think we can assume," said Geoffrey, "that Mavis was Pride – though Vanity might have been nearer the mark." Nigel allowed himself the ghost of a smile. "She wouldn't like that, of course; she'd never admit to it. She wouldn't want it to show in her portrait, either – hence her remark to Pennington about faces. And so," he went on, "that made five sins – all ready to hand, more or less. But then our author got stuck. It had been churchgoers till then, and he needed Anger. The Boyntons weren't church, but they had to do. And my guess is that he provoked the anger himself; I suspect it was he who rang the planning people. It would have been too pat, otherwise – anger turning up just when he needed it."

"He?" said Nigel.

"Well – I considered Pennington, of course. He's an odd bod. I don't know why he comes to church at all; half the time he just sits at the back and sketches. And he does take all those newspapers. He's not sufficiently interested in us, though, not as individuals; he just sees us as a lot of villagers. And he's supercilious, but not petty, or vindictive. No, it wasn't Pennington. I'm afraid it's more inconvenient than that." He paused. "It was Herbert."

"Herbert!" said Nigel, and now he did raise an eyebrow.

"It's Herbert who's been so obsessed with sin," said Geoffrey. "And look at my note – 'Disgraceful'. It's one of Herbert's words. He used it when we were discussing the letters. 'It's disgraceful!' he said. And then he looked as though he wished he hadn't. I suppose he didn't want Alice or me to make the connection. But that's what gave me the clue."

"So I sent him a reply," said Alice. "I shall never forgive myself."

"I was just as responsible," said Geoffrey. "I let you do it."

"I doubt if you could have stopped me. I cut out words, like Herbert, and pasted them down. I put 'WHAT ABOUT ENVY? IS THAT YOU?'. It was the one sin left – after Geoffrey had worked out Mavis. And then that poor man took an overdose. I shall never interfere in anything ever again." She looked stricken.

"It can't have been a very serious overdose," said Nigel.

"No," said Geoffrey, who had pointed this out already. "I do wonder, though, if he really was keeping Envy for himself. All that stuff about searching our hearts – he always included himself in it."

"But why envy?" said Nigel.

"Well – he's a churchwarden, a Lay Reader, in church terms he's a power in the land. But he's never *quite* been accepted, has he? We don't quite take him seriously. And I'm afraid a bit of it's the English class system."

Nigel looked a question.

"It doesn't seem to worry Abel Trevissick," said Alice, with whom Geoffrey had not shared this before.

"Abel," he said, " doesn't – 'know his place', exactly, but he's *sure* of his place, it doesn't bother him. Herbert is *un*sure, and he *is* bothered."

And there was more, he thought, which he could not say to Nigel. Herbert was just a small-time accountant, Nigel was clerk to a large practice. But other things would cut deeper. Nigel was gay – not a crime, but not straightforward either, in a village. Nigel had made a fool of himself over Frederick. Nigel had been accused of pilfering church funds. Herbert's life, so far as they knew, had been blameless. And yet somehow, in ways which Herbert would appreciate, it was Nigel who was accepted, and not himself.

"There's another thing," said Nigel. "Most of the charges in the letters were based on something."

"Not yours," said Geoffrey.

"The accusation was made. But the insinuation about the

two of you is –" (Geoffrey saw him search for the tactful word) "inappropriate."

"It was utterly silly," said Alice. "But I think we'd upset him. I challenged him over Original Sin, and when he returned to it the week after, you, Geoffrey – I think you may have dozed off."

"I always hope I look deeply contemplative," said Geoffrey. "But yes, I am drowsy in the mornings."

"There you are," said Alice. "I attacked one sermon, and you slept through the next. He was trying to get his own back."

"And the rest followed?" asked Nigel.

"Ours wouldn't have been the first," said Geoffrey. "I think it was Mavis. You remember how Herbert was all over her at first, and then it stopped? She probably gave him the brush-off; that's a much more likely stimulus. And so he decided that she was Pride – thinking herself too good for him, wanting to be admired – and he sent his letter. Then, perhaps, we annoyed him – and after that, the rest followed." And Nigel would have been next, he thought. The two churchwardens working together – and envy, simmering underneath… Then Septimus, perhaps; Herbert was not the first to accuse him of sloth. And Abel's increasing girth would have been another provocation; world poverty was one of Herbert's subjects. And even the Boyntons might have touched a nerve; apart from their wealth, Herbert would not look lightly on bending the rules. Then the shock of Alice's letter, the potentially tragic consequence…

The other two were looking at him, Geoffrey realised; he had wandered off. "But at what point the Seven Deadly Sins occurred to him," he said, "we shall probably never know, though my guess is – very early. Our 'sin', as you kindly remark, was not too aptly chosen; it makes more sense if he was trying to fit us into a preconceived pattern."

"Have you thought what we might do?" said Nigel.

"It's not up to me, thank goodness. You're the churchwarden, and the one with the legal knowledge. But I doubt if you can do anything without evidence; all we have, if you can call it that, is Herbert's supposed reaction to Alice's letter. There's not much to be gained by telling Septimus. He's obviously rather unbalanced; you'll just have to keep a careful eye on him."

"He's a bundle of insecurities, poor man," said Alice. We must try to be nicer to him."

They were gone, and it was off his hands. It had been trivial, a village storm in a teacup, and the only real sufferer had been Herbert, who could be said to have brought it on himself. But all that explanation had wearied him. Better to sit quiet and think about the good times. Accompanying, for instance. In their early days, he had played for Margery. Purcell's *Evening Hymn*, he remembered: *'Ev'n in thy arms...'* God's arms, of course. Still, he tried not to think of it after gin; it unmanned him.

He would be asleep soon, with no lunch; he wasn't used to pre-lunch drinking. Perhaps he would dream – of music and Margery. A musician silently, and to himself.

FABLES

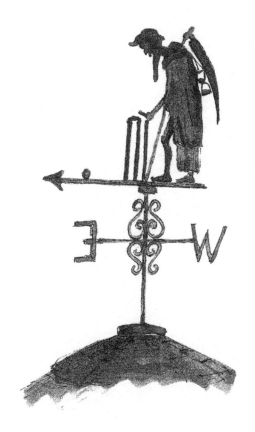

THE DEVIL AND KATE

IN THE old days, the Devil thought, it was straightforward. You offered a man everything he desired, provided you could have his soul in the end. The usual period was twenty years. They all fell for it, even the clever ones; they never really thought they'd have to pay. There was a man called – the Devil couldn't remember his name, but it began with an F, cleverer that most, reputedly. He asked for such silly things. And at the last, he had wriggled so delightfully. "I'll climb up to my God!" he had screamed out. Of course, he couldn't – poor, deluded fool. But it was fun to watch.

These days, no one really believed in the Devil, or in the soul much, either. You had to go about it a different way. You offered them something they thought they wanted, in exchange for something they thought they could do without. Then they found they couldn't. So you took away the original gift, and despair followed. They took to drink then, or suicide; in the best cases, they cursed God. And usually, it didn't take twenty years.

There was a cricketer called Henry Barnes; he was nineteen, and on one of the county staffs. His talent was fairly modest; the most he could hope for was a place in the county side, the life of a journeyman pro. But he wanted more. One night, the Devil came and tempted him. Henry Barnes had heard of the Devil, of course, but this was not quite what he'd expected. His Devil was no red creature with cloven hooves. He was a smooth gentleman, with sleek grey hair, and grey eyes set in an ageless face. He wore a pale grey suit, an immaculate white shirt, a darker grey tie with a diamond pin, and black patent-leather shoes. He spoke respectfully, like a well-trained servant, or upper secretary. He offered Henry Barnes as many runs as he wanted, provided that Henry would forswear love.

Henry Barnes did not quite believe that this was the Devil. He *said* he was, and certainly, he seemed to have appeared from nowhere. But then Henry had been asleep. He decided to treat it like the Lottery; expecting nothing, you bought your ticket anyway, just in case. There was no signing in blood, or anything of that sort; it was a gentleman's agreement, the Devil said. He left then, by the door.

And the next day, Henry began to score runs – lots of them. Batting was mainly a matter of hand-eye co-ordination, of getting into position early. And suddenly, he knew what to do; his *body* knew. Within a fortnight, he was in his county side; by the end of the season, he had topped the averages. He was the coming man.

Winter nets, some club cricket in Australia to keep in trim, and soon enough it was the start of the new season. Henry realised that he couldn't score hundreds all the time; he had to make lower scores, for verisimilitude: 34, 11, 3 – even the odd duck. It wasn't difficult. You purposely misjudged the line a fraction, and got bowled; you mistimed a lofted drive and were caught in the outfield. But for a few weeks at the start of the season, he pushed his luck. He scored so heavily, they had to pick him for England. And they did.

Meantime, there was a girl; she was called Kate. She lived two doors down from where he lodged. She was slim and fit-looking, with wavy brown hair. He liked being with her. You could not call it love; not even the Devil could call it that. They had hardly held hands. But she had a lovely smile. She was –

well, she was Kate. And she was coming to watch him play in his first Test.

The team gathered two days beforehand; there were introductions, nets. Some of them had been his childhood heroes; now they were colleagues. He played their bowling without difficulty.

On the evening before the Test, he went for a stroll – and suddenly, there was Kate in the street. It was chance. Her smile turned him over. He asked her back to the team hotel for a drink – and one thing led to another, as things do.

It was love all right, in its simplest, basic form. They had the most wonderful night, he thought, since the world began. They slept at last, and he let her go in the dawn, awake now to his responsibilities.

Breakfast, the coach to the ground; warm-ups, throw-downs. A brief net. It felt unreal. (He was, after all, a little short of sleep.) He was down to bat at three, his favourite position. A wicket fell. He was padded up; he could not say he was ready. Through the Long Room, down the steps past the members, onto the hallowed turf. It was like those dreams when something is hurtling towards you, and you cannot get out of the way. He was about to make a fool of himself, in front of his team-mates, his opponents, twenty-five thousand spectators, and the world. There was nothing he could do to stop it. He took guard.

The first ball was straight and a little short, and he played it easily. The next was fuller, on his legs; he pushed it wide of mid-on for a safe single. In the following over, he hit a four, cut hard behind point. Soon, he was into double figures. And gradually his nerves dropped away, and the tension eased out of him; it was like the sun on his back at the end of winter. By lunch, he had made fifty-seven; he reached his hundred on the dot of half past two. The crowd rose to him, a blur of applause. He was out soon after, genuinely beaten. Not *quite* the same, then – but good enough.

For the Devil, you see, did not really understand cricket. The best preparation consists of repeating the same movements over and over again, until they become instinct, part of the physical memory. For a year, the Devil had let him bat like the best in the world, and his body could not forget it, not all at once. He took steps to ensure that it never did. For the rest of his career, he practised assiduously, reinforcing the Devil's teaching, keeping the physical memory intact. His body let him down sometimes; there was a hamstring, and latterly, a knee. He did not have to get himself out; it happened naturally. The Press said he had lost his first fine, careless rapture. But the runs kept on coming. He had fifteen good years in the England side, and retired from all cricket aged thirty-seven, full of honour. Of course he married Kate. She is thicker-waisted now, but still has a lovely smile. There are two children.

As for the Devil, he had other fish to fry; there was a lot of frying in Hell. But this one had escaped his net, and it annoyed him. He would have to *do* something about cricket. For years they had been bowling at each other, rather than at the stumps, but they were so well padded that no one got hurt much. Words, then: perhaps he could persuade them to say unpleasant things – about each other's wives, mothers, race. The latter seemed particularly potent just now. Close fielders, whispering to the batsman…

They took to it eagerly; soon, it was part of the game. They had a mantra: 'What happens on the pitch stays on the pitch' – so almost no one was punished. They called it sledging; they thought they had invented it. But it was an invention of the Devil.

Two

THE UNICORN

THE UNICORN could just remember his mother. She had brought him up for a few months and then left him – for another part of the forest, he supposed, or perhaps for another forest altogether. He could not imagine a place that was not forest.

He had known no other unicorn, nor any other creature as large as he. Squirrels and rabbits scuttled about their busy lives, but they took little notice of him, or he of them. He was no threat; he was not carnivorous. He liked the birds better – bright red and green ones who squawked a lot, big black ones that flapped, and little brown ones whose song was the best of all.

And then there were men. They had never troubled him, but then they had hardly seen him. Something told him to keep away from them, and their dwellings, and he did.

As he grew older, he became aware of his horn. It was just a bump at first, but in time it grew longer, straighter, sharp-pointed. He grubbed the earth with it, prodded trees. He looked at his reflection in pools, proudly, curiously. He wondered what it was for. He was sure it was *for* something. It felt – well – horny.

One day, he approached a clearing; clearings meant men, but he was drawn to this one. A woman – a girl – was sitting on the ground quite near him; she seemed to be mending a pair of breeches. Her face was sad, not careworn, exactly, but as though she no longer cared about anything. And suddenly, he knew what he must do.

He had been standing behind some bushes; gently, he pushed aside the foliage and walked towards her, slowly. He did not want to frighten her. He stopped in front of her, knelt, and with bowed head lowered his horn into her lap. She put the breeches aside, but otherwise did not move. They stayed like that for some time. Then, almost absent-mindedly, it seemed, she began to rub the patch between his ears. It was soothing. They were made for each other.

The next thing he was aware of was the men – not through instinct, that was engaged elsewhere – but footsteps, voices. There were three of them, two younger ones and another who was much older. The unicorn got to his feet – it was a clumsy process – and galloped off into the trees, making a lot of noise. When he was sure they were not following, he stopped and retraced his steps, silently this time. He had never been part of a story before, and he wanted to know how it finished. Also, he was concerned about the girl.

He took up his original position behind the bushes, and watched.

"Virgin," one of them was saying. "It's how you catch a unicorn, remember? They'll always put their horn in a virgin's lap."

"Virgin," said his companion. He pointed to the older man. "'Ere," he said, "your wife's a virgin. Married six months, and still a virgin. Can't you do it, then?" He laughed, unpleasantly.

The older man grew red. Then he knocked the second speaker down. The fight was unfair, two against one. Fists, blood. It ended with the older man pinned to the ground. After the others had pummelled him a bit, they left. The beaten man got up, and trudged off. The girl's expression had never changed.

The unicorn crept away, too. He knew now what his horn

was for, but how could he use it if it caused such trouble? He was aware that animals killed other animals, but that was somehow dispassionate, necessary. This was so ugly. It was very worrying.

The next day, he went to the clearing again. Five girls this time, sitting on their heels, chattering; they looked as though they had been there for some time. He felt a sort of faithfulness to the earlier girl, but instinct told him it wasn't necessary. He pushed aside the bushes and peered at them. They looked back, uncertainly. Which to choose?

And then he thought: no more ugliness. With an effort of will, he turned and galloped off – but stopped when he heard the shouting. It was not at him, he was sure. He made his way back carefully, trying not to crack the twigs and pine cones. Two men, different ones, were standing over the girls.

"Five daughters between us," one was saying, "five – and not a virgin among 'em! One look at you lot, and he was off like a bleedin' arrow."

"What have you been up to?" said the other man.

A girl protested, weakly, but he slapped her face. Then he began unbuckling his belt.

The unicorn galloped off for good this time; he didn't want to know the rest. What was it with men, he wondered? He was used to this patch of the forest; he had grown up here. He liked the little brown birds, and the sun filtering through the branches. But the leaves blocked too much of it in summer, and in winter it was weak, and the days were short. Perhaps there was an elsewhere, where such things were not so. He might meet his mother again. Though he doubted whether she'd remember him.

Three

THE PICTURE

WHEN PIERO was nine, he was taken to see a relic; it was the index finger of St John the Baptist. He went with his father and mother, holding their hands, disconcerted among the jostling crowd. What he saw when his father lifted him was a small black stump, set upright in a gold, jewelled casket. He did not know what he was supposed to think. Set down, he studied faces. His mother's was full of wonder; she was a woman, he realised later, of easy piety. His father's face expressed nothing at all.

"How do they *know* it's the Baptist's?" he had asked afterwards. "How could it have survived for fourteen hundred years? And why has it still got black flesh on it?"

"It's a miracle," said his father.

"What's a miracle?"

"A miracle," his father said, "is something that creates faith, if we believe in it." And if we don't, Piero wondered? He didn't think his father had believed in it. He wasn't sure what he believed himself.

Years passed. His mother died, and he went to work with Maestro Domenico, a good teacher. Copying, filling in unimportant corners. Grinding the pigments, the stuff of their trade. Balance, measure and perspective. Finding himself.

Back home at last, he lived with his father, who was old and lonely. And a first commission: to paint the Baptist, at his culminating moment. A tree, he decided, with dark foliage; it was a tree that began it all. And the other tree behind. Otherwise, light – light from above, soft colours, pale shadows. To the left, three angels, rapt, like statuary. On the right, a man, bent over, turned away, removing his smock. The dove with wings extended, like one of the clouds. And beneath it, the central figure – solid, human, marble-skinned, hands in the act of prayer, the face of God. The Jordan behind, a suggestion only, reflecting sky and hills. And the Baptist: brown ragged tunic, left arm and fingers poised – so, the right hand reaching up with the bowl of Jordan water, to pour it over His head.

When it was done, after months, it was what he wanted. He knew it was good.

He called his father then; his father liked to be shown. He would shuffle in, stand too close because of his weak eyes, and peer at details, not seeing the whole. He was doing it now.

He stood back. "Piero," he said, "it is a miracle."

A still minute. Motes in sunbeams (how could you paint that?). For Piero, it had been self-belief, bending technique to the service of his vision. To the Priory of St John it was practical merely, a new altar-piece. But for his father, that sad sceptic (rheumy eyes, Jordan-coloured, grey hairs in his nostrils) – a miracle. Whatever he meant by it. But the words had been spoken.

That shrivelled digit might be genuine – for all Piero knew. But it was his picture which created faith.

FROM A ROYAL PECULIAR

THE OWL

THE PRECENTOR did not care for birds, nor for any other flying creatures. When he was a young priest, bats had got into his church. Bats were a protected species; humans weren't. The regulations were tortuous, and the mess was appalling; at times, the church was unusable. It was months before the bats could legally be got rid of.

So when the owl took up residence in Westminster Abbey, one dark day in late November, the Precentor had misgivings. The vergers, too, were slightly ambivalent – there was just a little mess. But everyone else thought it rather delightful. The owl mostly slept in the daytime, but woke for Evensong; the organ, in particular, got him going. He would swoop about in the upper reaches, and sometimes let out a melancholy hoot. The choir men (or Lay Vicars, as they were called) particularly enjoyed his company, and looked forward to his musical interruptions.

"Then nightly sings the mousing owl," said the Senior Lay Vicar (a bass), after the owl had hooted on two successive evenings.

"I think in the song it's 'the staring owl'," said William Pole (tenor), one of the youngest Lay Vicars, who had read English at university. "'Mousing owl' is from *Macbeth*."

"There can't be too many mice in here," said Ant leStrange (alto). "What do you think he eats?"

"Perhaps we ought to put out some birdseed."

"I don't think they eat birdseed."

"I expect he goes out at night, and flies back in again, He likes it here."

After a while, they thought they ought to mark his arrival. Gerald Crittall (alto) started them off. "*Love so amazing, so divine,*" he sang one Sunday morning, "*Demands my soul, my life, my OWL.*" Nick Johnson (tenor) on his immediate right, had to disguise his spluttering laugh as a cough; the Precentor did not approve of unseemly mirth. After that, they took their opportunities where they found them. The hymn *Owl for Jesus* was felt to be a particular success.

The Precentor was gaunt, grey-haired and long-faced. Though he was Head of the Choral Foundation, he did not really like musicians. They had agendas of their own, and an inappropriate, and largely incomprehensible, sense of humour. You never knew what they would be up to next. What did happen next was that Ralph Watson, the youthful Sub-Organist, improvised an Owl Fugue as a voluntary. It began with a four-note motif in dotted rhythm, a happy suggestion of 'To-whit, to-whoo'. The choir men grinned, and the Precentor noted it. Ralph had brought in a third voice by the time the choir procession had left the Abbey.

"I couldn't really do a whole fugue," he said afterwards, "but it did sound quite like one. The Precentor asked me what it was; I think he suspected something."

"What did you tell him?"

"I said it was by a Scandinavian, Wol Wolsen." The men, remembering their *Winnie the Pooh*, had taken to referring to the owl as 'Wol'.

"Did he believe you?"

"He believes anything if you say it with a straight face."

70

"Stupid man!" said Gerald. "No sense of humour, either." Gerald and the Precentor had crossed swords before.

Then the boys joined in. One of them turned round to Ant during a rehearsal.

"Mr. leStrange," he said, "it's a pity there aren't two owls."

"Why?"

"Because then they could sing *Owls in B minor,* and the Owls *Westminster Service.*"

"Oh, really!"

Next, the Organist and Master of the Choristers made an input. He was a most correct and proper person, a quite recent appointment, and what he did was not ostensibly improper at all. He changed the chant to Psalm 102. Verse 6, a Cantoris verse, reads, '*I am become like a pelican in the wilderness, and like an owl that is in the desert*'. The fourth quarter of the new chant went:

'And like an owl | that is | in the | desert...' A slight pause before the first bar-line produced a satisfying hoot on the alto crotchet, at the word 'owl'. Gerald Crittall went at it with a will, and the Decani men failed to contain their amusement.

Afterwards, the Precentor came up to the vestry. "I will *not* have this childish giggling in the choir stalls," he announced. "I've warned you about it before, and it's started again. If there is any repetition, the Dean and Chapter will take stern disciplinary measures."

"He only ever talks to us when we annoy him," said someone.

"He doesn't like Wol, either," said Ant. "He doesn't like any singers."

"Stern disciplinary measures!" said Gerald Crittall. "Sounds like Miss Whiplash to me. Bring her on!"

And finally, there was the Owl Sermon. They could never remember afterwards what the Dean's text had been, or what point his tale was supposed to illustrate; by Sunday Evensong, they were a little past attending to sermons. The tale, though, concerned a Sunday School teacher whose questions all seemed to require the same answer. One day, for a change, she brought the new curate with her.

"Now, children," he said. "Can anyone tell me: what has big black eyes, flies by night and makes a hooting sound?"

Silence.

"Come on, Jimmy," said the curate. "What do *you* think?"

"Well," said Jimmy, "I know it's got to be the little Lord Jesus. But it sounds like an owl to me."

Actually, they had heard the Dean tell this one before – but then it had been a squirrel.

Christmas came and went, and when the choir returned after their break, the owl was still with them. He caused less comment now, except from the congregation, who were mostly transient.

"Gee, Mr. Dean," an American would say, "do you know you have an owl loose in your Abbey?"

And the Dean would smile benignly, and say yes, he knew.

At last, one day in March, just after the start of British Summer Time, the owl was gone. A verger passed on the news when they arrived for Evensong.

"Well, he'd be lonely," said William Pole. "In spring, a young man's fancy turns to love."

"How do we know Wol's a man?" said Ant. No one had thought of this before.

"He sounds like an alto to me," said William.

"It's the same either way," said the Senior Lay Vicar. "I have heard that a young man's fancy turns in spring to what girls think about all the year round."

"What would you know about it?" said Gerald. The Senior Lay Vicar was both old and a bachelor.

No one thought much of Ant's suggestion. Wol was a bloke, they decided; he was one of themselves. It was good to think of him out in the world, enjoying life.

Though Gerald would always claim that the Precentor shot him.

Two

THE RING: A FANTASY

CANON WESTWOOD, making his way through the cloisters after Evensong, stopped by the Plague Stone and thought of the Lavender Lady. Westwood was in his late fifties, a spare figure, with a keen face, though there was kindness and potential amusement in the eyes. He was wearing a red cassock, of that peculiar hue permitted to royal establishments.

The Stone was a slab in the North Cloister floor, with an inscription:

*'DEAN STANLEY RECORDS THAT BENEATH THIS
STONE ARE INTERRED TWENTY-SIX
MONKS OF WESTMINSTER WHO DIED OF
THE BLACK DEATH IN 1348.'*

Stanley, a late-nineteenth-century Dean and an antiquarian, may well have been right, though in fact only one coffin was ever found there. An alternative tradition said it was the burial place of Long Meg of Westminster, a legendary giantess from Henry VIII's time, and indeed, the stone itself was sometimes known as 'Long Meg'. And there was a third, equally unlikely tale, a pendant to the Dean Stanley version, which Westwood had heard only recently.

The Lavender Lady was real enough, though. She was crone-like, increasingly bent, with rather swarthy wrinkled skin, bright eyes, and straggly grey hair under a dull brown shawl. For years, she had stood on the same spot by the Plague Stone. "50p for a bunch of Lavender," she would say to the tourists. For him, and the rest of the Chapter, she had a deferential smile and the sketch of a curtsey – as though, he thought, she were an old family retainer. Somehow, she had become part of the scenery. He remembered the vergers over their coffee once, wondering what they would do if John the Baptist came to the Abbey, straight from the wilderness. Turn him out as a vagrant, they thought, probably. The Lavender Lady was less obtrusive. Nevertheless, there had been colleagues who wanted to turn *her* out; she was untidy, an anomaly, and she presumed too much on a sort of squatter's right. It was the Dean who pointed out that turning people away was hardly their business – quite apart from the bad publicity. Westwood had not seen her for a while now. He wondered what had happened to her, whether they had some pastoral responsibility. But he put the thought aside; there were too many pressing claims on his attention.

William Pole, Lay Vicar of Westminster Abbey, had arranged to meet Sophie in St James's Park, on one of their usual benches by the pond. William was in his mid-twenties, though his fresh face and mop of brown hair gave him the look of a schoolboy still. He had met Sophie when she came to the Abbey to hear some Josquin; she was finishing a PhD in Renaissance music. In the meantime, she was temping in an office, and this was her lunch hour. Her slight figure, and elfin face as she turned to greet him, were becoming increasingly familiar to him, but seeing her afresh still brought a frisson of excitement, and strangeness. She had told him fairly little about her background; he had gathered her parents were dead. But early in their acquaintance, she had astonished him. One day after Evensong, instead of making for Victoria Street, as they usually did, she had led him along the North Cloister – and had spoken to Lavender Lil.

"Hello, Auntie," she said.

"Hello, my honey."

And then had she introduced William. Lavender Lil (whose name wasn't Lil at all) had given him a clear-eyed look, as she took his hand in both of hers. He felt as though he were passing some sort of test.

"Is she really your aunt?" he had asked afterwards.

"My great aunt," said Sophie, "my only relation. She doesn't like me talking to her here, but I wanted you to meet her."

"Do you see her much?"

"From time to time. She lives in a flat in Brixton; she's a gypsy. So am I, I suppose…" They had the same brown eyes, he realised, and Auntie's straggling grey hair must once have been as black as Sophie's. A gypsy… It added to her sense of otherness. He had resolved to speak to Auntie whenever he passed her, but he had hardly seen her since. She had been ill, apparently, in hospital. Sophie was worried about her, and wanted to talk.

"Auntie was never a Traveller," she was saying now, throwing a bit of crust at a couple of ducks. "Her parents lived in a house. But she knows all sorts of things – tea-leaves, herbal remedies. Gypsy stuff. Once, she read my palm: I'm to be lucky in love, and find a fortune."

William considered it, as she finished her sandwich. He was beginning to think that life without her might be unimaginable. They had never talked about love. Was her remark entirely innocent? What had she meant by it?

"That'd be nice," he said.

Canon Parry-Jones, the Canon in Residence, was reading the Second Lesson; it was the Parable of the Talents. Parry-Jones was large and bull-necked, with a red face and a domineering voice; he was a rather hard-line Evangelical. Canon Westwood, who liked Parry-Jones's voice as little as his opinions, was choosing to let his mind wander and think about something else. And principally, about the Abbey's finances.

Terrorist activity in London had reduced their tourist income, and they could not any longer draw on their reserves. One or two pet projects would have to be abandoned, and all expense carefully scrutinised. It was Westwood's job, as Canon Treasurer, to spell this out, and he knew that not all his colleagues were prepared for it. There would be distress, and people fighting their corners. Parry-Jones, for one... Well, they were used to his talking at them, and not listening. Parry-Jones was grinding to a conclusion. *"There shall be weeping and gnashing of teeth"*; he was enjoying that, Westwood thought. It would be a relief to stand for the choir's *Nunc Dimittis*. Westwood knew he did not understand music but, in Beecham's phrase, he liked the noise it made.

William, in his place in the choir stalls, had also noted Parry-Jones's grim relish. The choir were on good terms with the Dean and Chapter, but they had rather taken against Parry-Jones after the incident of the croquet match – Lay Vicars versus Canons, in the College Garden. Parry-Jones, having 'practised beforehand, which spoils all the fun', as the Flanders and Swann song had it, had turned up in an absurd back-to-front baseball cap, and had then gone off in a bit of a huff when he lost. William wondered if Parry-Jones knew the 'teeth-gnashing' joke, the old man's reply to the hell-fire preacher.

"But some of us haven't *got* any teeth."

Preacher (with venom): "Teeth will be provided!"

But what had struck William more was an earlier verse of the parable – because of what Sophie had told him that lunchtime. They had agreed to meet in the park as usual, and he had known, the moment he saw her, that she was upset.

"It's Auntie," she said, as soon as he sat down. "You know she was in hospital? Well, she died last night."

He reached out a hand; he had not known her vulnerable.

"I was with her yesterday," Sophie went on; "she was very weak and rambling. She told me strange things." He waited. "She said that a long time ago, we were very rich. One of us married one of the quality here – I think she meant a Canon – or at any rate lived with him, and they went abroad and were very grand. They'd found some treasure under a stone. I asked her which stone, and she said the Plague Stone, the one she always stood by. Though she didn't call it that; she couldn't read, you know. She even knew the Canon's name; he was a Dr. Bull. Then it got even odder. She said that there's treasure there still, but you're only supposed to dig it up in great need; it's unlucky otherwise. Gypsies don't like to cross their luck..." She trailed away.

Buried treasure, he thought, like a children's story. They'd have had to lever the Stone up – and put it back.

"How did she know all this?"

"Her gran told her."

"Sophie..." He wasn't sure how far he should press her. "Do you believe it?"

"No. I don't think so. Poor Auntie."

And poor Sophie, he thought; her last relation gone. She had leaned her head on his shoulder then, for comfort, a new experience. But what he had noticed, listening to Parry-Jones, was the third man in the parable, the one who had buried his treasure in the ground so that he – or someone else? – could retrieve it later. He did not think of it as a portent, exactly; he did not believe in the tale, any more than Sophie had. But it would be something to tell her; it might divert her. And he would do a small piece of research first.

The Abbey library was in the West Cloister, just round the corner from the Plague Stone; the librarian, who liked this sort of query, was most helpful. A computer search revealed no Dr. Bull, but there was an interesting Canon Bullivant. In 1817, it appeared, having come into an unexpected inheritance, he had resigned suddenly and gone to live in Italy. Contemporary rumour suggested a woman in the case. Here was something more definite to tell Sophie. It was raining, so they agreed to meet in Starbucks, and spin out coffee and muffins as long as they could.

"Inheritance, my eye," said Sophie, when he had finished. "They dug up the treasure from under the stone – and sold it." It was clear now that she wanted to believe it.

"It wouldn't have been the same stone," he said. "The current one was placed there well after Bullivant's time. But if there really was treasure, who would have put it there?"

She thought. "What about the Dissolution of the Monasteries? The Abbey was Benedictine, wasn't it? The old guard would have wanted to keep at least some of their treasures. Henry VIII was utterly rapacious; he laid hands on anything he could get."

"So you're saying the monks hid them?"

"People hid all sorts of things. It was a crime to keep pre-Reformation church music; you were supposed to destroy it all. But when Mary became Queen, out it came again. Choirmen had part-books from the Old Hall Manuscript, and the Eton Choir Book, and so on, stashed in their lofts. Well, you would, wouldn't you? Then they sold them back to the Dean and Chapter. Nice little earner."

"But – the treasure must have been there for hundreds of years. And how would anyone know it was still there?"

"Oh, it's not difficult to leave clues behind you. What was yesterday's anthem?"

"Byrd, *Civitas sancti tui. 'Jerusalem desolata est…'*" It was one of his favourites.

"I thought so. Well, there you are: 'Jerusalem' is the Jerusalem Chamber, where the Abbey plate was kept, and it's desolate because the stuff's been taken away." The Jerusalem Chamber was the huge, oak-vaulted ex-Abbot's dining room where

Henry IV had died, and parts of the Authorised Version were translated.

"Old Byrd'll probably tell you where it's hidden," she went on, "if you look hard enough."

"Sophie…"

"Byrd was a closet Catholic. Of course he'd want to preserve the Benedictine treasure."

"Are you serious?"

"No, I'm making it up. All I'm saying is, there are plenty of ways to keep a secret going."

The rain was trickling down the window still. But it was good, he thought, to see her more cheerful.

Canon Westwood's first degree was in Chemistry; he had also been an Archdeacon. He was a practical man. But he had a vein of whimsy, and an almost schoolboy sense of the ridiculous; you could see it in the wrinkles round his eyes. Walking back from Evensong again, he remembered the third Plague Stone story, the one the Dean had told over drinks last week. In 1536, the Dean said, the monks, fearing they were about to be dissolved, had buried much of their plate in the Abbey grounds. There was no record of its ever being dug up. He then suggested that they had hidden it under the site of the Plague Stone, since no one would have wanted to search an old plague pit. He half-hinted that it was still there. Westwood dimly remembered hearing the tale before – but not the bit about the plague pit. Where had the Dean got it from? He wondered whether the Dean had made it up – particularly as Parry-Jones, who was Welsh, had been pontificating about the origins of legends. Was the Dean trying to originate a legend of his own? Or was he merely pulling Parry-Jones's leg? The Dean was a slightly remote figure, with the driest sense of humour; he would occasionally make brief, deadpan remarks – not so much to prick Parry-Jones's bubble, because Parry-Jones never noticed, but for the benefit of those who understood. Westwood never dared to catch the Dean's eye at these moments. Of course there was no treasure under the Plague Stone; it was about as likely as finding the bones of Long Meg, the legendary giantess. But supposing there had been, there would need to be a hollow space for it. Whether you could detect hollows under slabs of stone, he was uncertain; possibly not. Nevertheless, for his own purposes he would sally forth towards midnight, armed with his hammer, and tap the Stone a bit, and the one next to it. Then he would walk the few yards back to his house and pour himself a whisky. He *could* just pretend that he had done it – but this way was more fun. For the point was to tell the Dean about it afterwards, with a face as deadpan as the Dean's own. An attempt, he would claim, to restore the Abbey's finances. The Dean would give him a long look, and say nothing; but he would know that his invention had been rumbled. The Dean – though he would not admit to it – also had a sense of the ridiculous.

William and Sophie, meanwhile, were sitting in The Buckingham, where William and the beer were spinning a quiet fantasy: if Bullivant could raid the hoard for the sake of his gypsy, why shouldn't he, William, do the same? Leaning closer because of the noise of the drinkers, he tried it out on Sophie.

She gave him a gypsy answer. "You're only supposed to do it in great need," she told him. "Auntie said so. It's unlucky otherwise."

"We're in as much need as Bullivant ever was; we need the deposit for a flat." They had talked briefly about living together, but Sophie had yet to agree to it.

She sailed past these implications. "Well, if there *is* anything there," she said, "it has to be hollow. Tap it and find out."

"I can't just go tapping bits of the cloister with my ear to the ground. People will think I'm mad."

"Do it at night, then. Kip in the Lay Vicars' vestry."

"Sophie…" It was only supposed to be fantasy, he wanted

to tell her. What had they to go on? Bullivant was real enough. Beyond that, there was the deathbed tale of an ignorant old woman, Sophie's improbable guess about the Dissolution, and two rather tenuous coincidences: the man in the parable, and Byrd's *'Jerusalem desolata est'*. But there would be no harm in just tapping, he realised. Sophie wanted him to. It would be an adventure, something to talk about afterwards. Also (he almost hugged himself) she hadn't argued with him about the flat.

And so it was that parallel lines met. The discomfort of the vestry floor reminded William of another Biblical joke for Parry-Jones. It was the sign over the church crèche: *We shall not all sleep, but we shall all be changed*. He did not think he would get much sleep here. Big Ben struck midnight then, and it was soon after that he heard the tapping. The men's vestry was on the first floor, and the noises were beneath him, in the cloisters – metal on stone. Tap, tap, tap; pause; tap, tap, tap. He crept downstairs and listened again; the noises, he thought, were a good thirty yards off. He eased open the huge Song School door, hoping it wouldn't creak, but it was quite silent. Then he went onto all fours – and peeped.

Someone was at the other end of the North Cloister, someone with a torch. As it moved, William saw his face; it was Canon Westwood. He stood up, and with a rather French gesture, appeared to spread his hands and shrug his shoulders.

Footsteps next, from the Little Cloister direction, where the Canons lived. A stone bench projected from the cloister wall, and William ducked behind it.

"Westwood!" Parry-Jones's voice. "What are you doing? You're disturbing my work."

Parry-Jones's front door was in a passage called the Dark Cloister, nearer to the Plague Stone than the others. As Canon Theologian, he turned out theological works at a furious rate. Presumably he burnt the midnight oil – with the window open.

William did not catch Westwood's reply, but he heard Parry-Jones's "Ridiculous nonsense!" as he stumped off towards his house. Westwood left more quietly then, and William crept back behind the door.

He let an hour go by before his own investigation. His hammer was lighter and less noisy than Westwood's, and after trying the Plague Stone, he chose another nearer to the Song School. Then he got up and shrugged, too. It seemed to be the appropriate response.

He told Sophie about it the next evening, sitting in her small, rented flat. There was a work-table with books and a laptop, two shabby armchairs, and a gas fire with a meter. A little treasure, he thought, might have gone a long way.

He began with Westwood and Parry-Jones, and went on to his own findings. "I used Muzio Clementi for comparison," he said, "because his stone was farther from Parry-Jones's house. But they both made the same dull sound."

"That'll be Clementi," said Sophie, who had had to learn a Clementi sonata at school. "But what do you think Westwood was doing there?"

"I've thought about that," said William. "Auntie would have had the gypsy take on the treasure story, which must have originated with Bullivant's mistress. But suppose there was a much older, Abbey version? That's how Bullivant would have known about it – and Westwood." And as he said it, he almost half-believed it.

"Yes," she said. "Bit of a coincidence, though, Westwood turning up on the same night. Pity we can't ask him why."

But William was expanding on his theory. "Sophie… if Auntie's tale really was a family secret, then that means you're descended from Bullivant's gypsy – Bullivant, too, possibly. Had you thought of it?"

"Yes," she said gently. "And Auntie, too. Poor Auntie – all those years guarding her treasure, and when she was dying she passed the secret on. I'm the last in the line. Not that I suppose there is any treasure; Bullivant would have had it all. Why would he leave any?"

"You believe in Bullivant's treasure, then?"

"I've something to show you," she said. She began rootling around in her handbag; he never knew what women kept in handbags. Her intent look contracted his heart.

She found her purse, took something out of it. "It's Auntie's ring," she said. "They give you the ring after a cremation. She always wore it, and I never thought about it."

It was large, as though made for a man, gold apparently, and worn with age. There was a small crater where the only gem had been roughly gouged from its setting, though not recently.

"What do you think?" she said.

He knew what she wanted him to think: that this was part of the monks' hoard, dug up by Bullivant, presented to his gypsy mistress, and passed down in her family ever since. And at some stage, the gem gouged out and sold.

"The Abbot's ring?" he suggested, wishing it were true, for her sake.

"We'd have to take it to an expert," Sophie said.

He thought about it. "No, don't let's. If it *is* the real thing, we'd feel bound to give it back, and if not, we'd only be disappointed. Keep it, Sophie; it's an heirloom, a piece of family history. You can tell your grandchildren about it." He paused, tentative, a little self-conscious; the ring lay in his palm. "Or ours," he said, "if you'll have me."

CHRISTMAS SUPPLEMENT

Ballad

The trees within the garden
Were beckoning and tall,
And one that bore an apple
Was fairest of them all.

The serpent in the garden
Has lifted up his head:
"Eat of the Tree of Knowledge
And be a God," he said.

And Eve has plucked the apple
And held it in her hand,
And Adam in his blindness
Has blinked at God's command.

And they have left the garden,
It was a shame to see,
And God has sent the Son of Man
Who hangs upon a tree.

All glory to the Father,
And to his only Son,
And glory to the Holy Ghost,
The Comforter. Amen.

Shepherds

How should we, belated, tiring,
Wonder-struck with sudden light,
Find the lamb of man's desiring
In the wilderness of night?

Keep we to our ancient calling,
Mark the anguished yeanling's cry,
Let the voices, soaring, falling,
Trumpet peace to distant sky.

Joseph

I cannot hold a candle
To such a one as he,
The God my love would dandle
Upon her human knee.

The darkness in the stable
Leaves me at peace, alone.
I do what I am able.
I take them for my own.

Mary

We thought you safe in the strawy manger,
But lift you, drawn by a dream of danger,
To look for a crib where you'll seem a stranger.

So sleep now on my aching shoulder
While the donkey plods, and never be older,
But warm, close, as the years grow colder.

Lullaby

Sleep, sleep,
Old as the world,
Into an ancient
Evil hurled,
Fresh from the womb
And foetus-curled.

Sleep, sleep on –
And wake from dreaming,
Live to be real
In a seethe of seeming,
And die, broken,
Mocked, redeeming.

NOTES

The Picture. Piero della Francesca's *Baptism of Christ* is in The National Gallery, London.

The Owl. *'Owls in B minor'*, etc.: i.e. Herbert Howells (1892-1983), prolific composer of church music.